MW00771967

STONE COLD

A GIA SANTELLA CRIME THRILLER
BOOK 8

KRISTI BELCAMINO

LIQUID MIND PUBLISHING

Liquid Mind Publishing
This is a work of fiction. All characters, names, places and events are the product of the author's imagination or used fictitiously.

GIA SANTELLA CRIME THRILLER SERIES

Enjoying the Gia Santella series? Scan below to order more books today!

Vendetta

Vigilante

Vengeance

Black Widow

Day of the Dead

Border Line

Night Fall

Stone Cold

Cold as Death

Cold Blooded

Dark Shadows

Dark Vengeance

Dark Justice

Deadly Justice

Deadly Lies

PROLOGUE

It was the first time he'd made a public appearance in years, and the people of Mexico could hardly believe it. They lined the street in a thick mass barely held back from the passing funeral procession by Mexico City police standing in a human chain.

The black limousine crawled along behind the hearse, hampered by heavily armed SWAT team members on foot, surrounding the vehicles and creating a wall of protection four men deep.

Fights broke out as the vehicles passed. Those who viewed *El Jefe Grande* as a benevolent saint went head to head with those who considered him a stone-cold killer— *asesino a piedra fría.*

On the rooftops lining the main thoroughfare, sharpshooters from three different police departments were spread out, searching for anyone who might intend harm to the occupants of the limousine.

Inside the vehicle, behind dark-tinted, bulletproof windows, Nico Ortiz Morales, aka *El Jefe*, looked out at the people and felt numb.

He didn't flinch when a man with a gun broke through the

police line at one corner and made it all the way over to the window before a SWAT member shot him dead, flecks of brain and blood spatter landing on the window.

At that moment, he wondered if his heart had died along with his wife.

He'd loved her more than anything else in his world.

And yet that love had not saved her.

She'd killed herself anyway. Her beautiful body found splayed out like a virgin in their wedding bed. He couldn't help but imagine her in front of her vanity, carefully applying her makeup while he was on business in the dark reaches of the jungle. While he was building his drug empire, she was pulling on her silky wedding gown that still fit after fifteen years and penning the note that would shatter the remains of his broken heart.

While he was speaking to coca farmers in Columbia about cocaine, she was pouring herself a glass of their most expensive wine from their estate's cellar. She ordered the house staff not to disturb her, and then she proceeded to empty the prescription bottle into her mouth. She had not even finished the glass of wine before she lay dead on their bed, clutching the wedding ring she'd removed from her finger.

He'd returned home to find her body. It was later, after the coroner had come and taken her away, that he had found the note on the nightstand. She'd always been a romantic and had sealed it with red wax.

He'd ripped it open carelessly. It had taken him two attempts to comprehend what he was reading.

She could no longer live with the guilt of betrayal. She'd betrayed him not once, but twice.

Most recently, she'd betrayed him by embarking on a year-long affair with a young Parisian fashion designer she'd been secretly financing. The young man had killed himself when she'd broken off the relationship earlier in the week.

The second confession was by far the worst betrayal.

She'd lied about the death of his daughter.

In the end, it was why he'd ordered her burial in a plot in Mexico City away from his own family plot.

And yet, still he'd mourn her publicly and attend her spectacular funeral mass at the largest Catholic church in Mexico City. It would be a service befitting the wife of someone of his status. The public would expect no less.

But once he'd honored her with a funeral mass worthy of her position as his wife, he would never allow himself to grieve for her again.

She'd tainted his love and grief by the second confession. The one she'd seemed to add in at the last minute as if it were a postscript.

And fool woman that she was, she hadn't even realized that the second confession would be the one that brought him to his knees. He could have lived with her affair. After all, she'd once forgiven him for the same transgression.

But the second secret—the one she'd kept from him for the past two years—had been the ultimate betrayal.

It was unforgivable.

His daughter—his own flesh and blood—was not dead as she'd told him two years ago.

The child was alive.

And living in San Francisco.

Her name was Rosalie.

1

ROSALIE SHUFFLED THE PLAYING CARDS, EXPERTLY EXECUTING A one-handed shuffle that would make any Vegas dealer proud. She then dealt the cards with precision, each card lying perfectly on top of the one thrown before it.

Dante waited until all of his cards were before him on the black oak table before he scooped them up and gave me a look, raising his eyebrow.

"What?" I said.

"You guys play poker a lot?"

"Maybe. Got a problem with that?"

"I'm not sure it's appropriate for a nine-year-old to be a card shark, that's all."

"Oh, don't be such an old man," I said. "Besides, it's card sharp."

"Sharp?"

"Sharp."

"It's not shark?"

"Nope," I said.

"That's dumb." He rolled his eyes.

Rosalie laughed. It was wonderful to see her so lighthearted.

This was a far cry from the kid who'd crawled into the back of my Jeep two years ago with ICE agents chasing after her.

She'd seen loved ones raped and murdered, witnessing worse violence than most hard-core gang members serving in San Quentin.

"After this game, can we show Dante our card trick?" she asked, not taking her gaze off the cards she held splayed in her hand.

"Most definitely," I said.

My friend, Danny, the best hacker in San Francisco, had taught her a crazy cool card trick. She loved showing it off.

Later, after Rosalie had taken all our quarters at poker and shown Dante her card trick, I'd sent her to bed with Django, the Pitbull-mix dog who used to be mine.

Once I heard both Rosalie and the dog snoring in her bedroom, Dante and I headed to the rooftop of the loft.

It was summer in San Francisco—which meant, of course, that it was freezing—so I lit both heat lamps, and we wrapped ourselves in thick blankets as we sprawled in the lounge chairs under my grape arbor.

In the distance, to the east, I could see the glow of the Bay Bridge beyond the downtown skyscrapers dotted with white lights.

The sky to the west looked turbulent, a roiling gray and black mass.

"Storm's coming in," Dante said, looking the same way.

"Glad you're staying over."

Dante lived in Calistoga but was down in the city for a board meeting for my company, Ethel's Place.

Ethel's Place, named after my friend who was murdered, helped homeless people who wanted to get back into society. We built multi-use buildings that offered apartments upstairs and retail shops on the street level where the residents could work and train for up to a year—getting them off the streets, employing them, and giving them skills to set out on their own later on.

After getting the business up and running, I was basically a figurehead on the board but still tried to attend quarterly meetings.

I knew Dante always felt torn leaving his restaurants, but I was selfish and wanted his company, so I begged him to come down for the meeting early and stay the night.

We'd taken Rosalie to dinner at some hip, up-and-coming restaurant Dante had wanted to do recon on. "Not bad," had been his verdict after we'd shelled out three hundred bucks for three tiny meals of unidentifiable foods. I'd had to drive through Mickey D's after so Rosalie would actually have some food in her before bed.

Huddled under blankets on my roof, I reached over to a small, jeweled box I'd hidden in the palm plant and extracted a small joint. I puffed on it a few times and passed it to Dante.

"Rosalie's a great kid," he said.

I beamed in the dark. "I know, right?"

"Does she ever talk about James?"

"Sure," I said. "She goes over there sometimes."

"She does?"

"Yeah. Well, every Thursday. Why do you act so surprised?"

James was my ex-boyfriend. When Rosalie had first come into my life, I'd been with James, and for a while, we'd been a family.

Until he dumped me.

I grabbed the joint from Dante and inhaled. Only after I exhaled did I speak.

"He just had a kid."

It was the first time I'd said the words out loud, and it hurt less than I'd thought it would.

"Really?" Dante said.

When James had been shot and paralyzed by his own colleagues on the San Francisco Police Department, the doctors had questioned whether he'd ever be able to have children or even walk again. He'd undergone some experimental stem cell treatment overseas after we'd broken up, and, though he still used a wheelchair, he was regaining feeling and limited use of his legs. While his manhood had still been, uh, very, very functional after the accident, his baby-making ability had been in doubt. Until now, I guess.

"Good for him."

"Yeah." I was quiet.

"You okay with all that?"

"I guess." I stubbed out the joint.

"Gia?"

"I still love him. I want him to be happy. That's what real grown up love is, right?"

Dante gave a bitter laugh. "Yeah."

"Well, it sucks."

We both burst out laughing.

One fateful night a few years back, we'd both lost everything to murderers. Dante lost his husband of only a few hours, Matt. I'd lost my boyfriend, Bobby.

Now, we both sat in silence. We'd been best friends for so long that it didn't take words for me to know we were both remembering that horrific night.

"I guess I'm destined to be alone forever," I said.

Dante surprised me by jumping up and slipping under the blanket with me on my chaise lounge. He laid his head on my shoulder and whispered. "Silly, Gia. You have me. You'll never be alone. Not as long as I walk this earth."

Leaning down, I kissed his brow.

He was right.

I was the luckiest girl in the world.

"Do you think Rosalie will grow up and take care of us when we're old?" I said.

"Uh, yeah. Duh," he said. "We're going to be two doddering old fools drinking our whiskey sours, and she's going to be our boss, scolding us not to drink and smoke weed. And we'll just cackle with laughter."

I got caught up in the fantasy.

"Can we live on the beach?"

"Yes!"

"And Rosalie will have kids, so in a way we'll be like grand-parents, right?"

"Of course!" Dante said. "We'll be the coolest grandparents ever. We'll tell them stories about how naughty we were when we were their age!"

"Oh, we better not!" I said.

"Oh, we *will*!"

I closed my eyes, imagining a life many years down the road when I was a gray-haired grandma in a rocking chair at a beach house watching children play in the waves in front of me and sipping my cocktail as the sun set.

My reverie was interrupted by a loud alarm on my phone.

Somebody was at the front door downstairs. I jumped up in surprise.

Nobody should have been able to get that far inside my building without other alarms going off.

I quickly grabbed the phone and clicked to the camera outside my steel front door. It was an older woman whom I didn't recognize. How in the hell had she gotten into the building?

I was up and down the stairs with Dante at my heels.

Once down in the loft, I reached up into my closet and extracted my Glock from the gun safe before I ordered Dante into Rosalie's bedroom. "Go in and lock that door until I call for you."

He didn't argue.

2

IT HAD ALL UNFURLED ACCORDING TO HIS PLANS.

It was nearly over.

Patience and persistence had gotten him this far.

It would serve him to the end.

And then he would be free.

Only a few more pieces of the puzzle and everything would fall into place.

His loyalty, his tenacity, his superior intelligence, would all be recognized and rewarded.

Soon.

For now, though, it was business as usual.

3

Nico Morales bowed his head as he placed a single pink rose on his wife's gold coffin, pausing as the flashbulbs from the approved paparazzi captured the moment for perpetuity.

He lifted his head, flashing black eyes meeting those of the two photographers who stopped and nodded, handing their cameras to two of his men. The men peered at the images through the viewfinder. They would delete any that showed Nico's face clearly.

The two photographers were the only people who had been allowed to point a camera toward Nico for the past decade. One worked for the BBC, the other for the Associated Press. Both had proven they could be trusted to photograph the graveside events in the way that Nico had dictated.

The only other people attending the burial were Nico's attorney and confidant, Anthony Perez, and his late wife's elderly mother who was escorted by his sister-in-law. She glared at him the entire mass.

After placing the rose on the casket, Nico turned and headed toward the limousine.

If anybody noticed his eyes were bone dry, no comment was made.

As soon as Nico was back inside his heavily guarded compound in the hills miles above Mexico City, he changed out of his suit into some worn jeans and a soft black button down shirt. He lit a Mayan Sicars cigar and poured some Michter's bourbon into a crystal tumbler. He tugged on the cigar for a few seconds and then, while he exhaled, swirled the amber liquid around before taking a deep gulp.

The fiery alcohol slipping down his throat temporarily shook off the sense of numbness that had pervaded him since he'd found his wife's body and the note.

He pushed a button and summoned Anthony.

The older man, still in his Brioni suit from the funeral mass, appeared moments later, his reading glasses propped up on the thinning gray hair on top of his head.

Nico gestured for him to sit down in the light brown leather chair that matched the one Nico was in. He poured the attorney some of the bourbon and handed him a cigar. Neither man spoke.

Only after Anthony had sipped some bourbon and smoked some of the cigar did Nico hand him Sylvia's suicide note. The older man read silently for a few minutes and then folded the note back in half.

"She is lucky she killed herself," he said. "If I would've learned of this before her death, she would have begged me for death by fire."

Nico frowned. The comment was harsh. Even though she'd broken his heart with her suicide and the news in the note, he couldn't deny that he'd loved her.

"She was my wife."

"During the autopsy they found an IUD," Anthony said,

keeping his eyes on the tip of the cigar as he examined the ember there.

Nico winced as if in pain.

Anthony was possibly the only person who knew that the couple had tried fruitlessly for more than a decade to conceive. It had always been Nico's greatest wish to be a father.

When it became clear that they would not conceive, Nico confessed to Sylvia that he already did have a daughter. Her name was Rosalie. She had been conceived years ago when he had first been married to Sylvia. He'd gone back to visit family in Guatemala and had an affair with a local woman. After he'd learned the woman had borne a baby out of their union, Nico had sent his soldiers to get the baby, but they had failed. A group of villagers had armed themselves, and a shoot-out had occurred. The mother of his child was killed in the crossfire. It was a terrible tragedy and the worst possible outcome.

The guilt of leaving the infant motherless along with the guilt of cheating on Sylvia had overcome Nico. He'd backed off and left the child alone to be raised by her grandmother. Until that day when Sylvia said she could not have children.

After begging Sylvia forgiveness for the affair, Nico said he'd recently gotten word that the girl was on her way to the United States. She might, in fact, already be there. He wanted Sylvia's permission to bring the girl back to their home so they could raise her as their own.

To his surprise, Sylvia said that not only was it a wonderful idea but also that she would personally fly to California to meet the girl and bring her back to Mexico safely. Such a precious and important package could not be left to the lackeys who worked for Nico in the states, she said.

At her words, Nico thought he could not possibly love her more.

Anthony advised against it. When Nico disagreed, Anthony insisted on going to California to oversee the hand-off.

Meanwhile, Nico stayed home running the daily operations of his massive cartel, which were surprisingly similar to the tasks of the CEO of a Fortune 500 company. Dealing with supply issues, personnel issues, taxes, manufacturing snafus ... the list went on and on. Nico learned early on the importance of delegating, so it wasn't as overwhelming as it could have been. But it kept him busy. Despite this, he spent the entire time that Sylvia and Anthony were gone in nervous anticipation.

It was only when Sylvia walked into their Mexican fortress alone that he learned what had happened. His daughter had been killed when one of his men—a Mexican-American named Garcia—had drawn attention from authorities cracking down on a child-trafficking ring.

Garcia, behind his back, had been selling unaccompanied children who crossed the border into America. If Garcia hadn't already been dead, Nico would've flown to San Diego himself, risking the loss of everything, just to strangle the man with his own bare hands. The fury was nearly impossible to stifle. And underneath it lay a deep shame that he had entrusted so much to a fool.

Along with the crushing blow of learning his daughter was dead, Nico was beside himself that a man under his reign had been abusing and harming children. His own dead mother's love may not have stopped him from being a criminal, but it would ensure he never harmed a hair on any child's head.

Each year, he anonymously donated $2 million to organizations that helped children in his country. He tried to keep it secret, but rumors had swirled after one particularly large donation. That was why, despite being the most powerful drug lord possibly in the world, old women in Mexican churches still knelt to pray for his soul every day, working their worn and smooth rosaries through gnarled fingers and asking the dear Lord to bless Nico Morales.

But all of it had been a lie.

His marriage now seemed like a farce.

For years, Sylvia had taken to her bed and cried each month when her period came.

Now he knew that, years before, she'd secretly undergone surgery to have an IUD implanted.

Marriage was based on trust.

She'd lied to him for years. And she'd lied to him about Rosalie being dead. She'd sat there stonily and watched him grieve for a daughter he would never meet.

It was unconscionable.

The woman must never have loved him.

And in some ways that hurt the most.

4

I STUDIED THE WOMAN ON MY LAPTOP SCREEN. THERE WAS nothing familiar about her. And she wasn't trying to hide her face, instead looking right up at the camera pointing down at her.

But the fact was that somehow this woman had gotten into my secure building without any alarms sounding and made it to the fourth floor, ringing the fucking doorbell at midnight like it was a social visit.

If I hadn't known better, the woman would have come across as a doddering grandmotherly type. She had on slacks, ballet flats, a cardigan sweater, and wire-rimmed glasses. But I could tell by the way the woman stood, poised and alert, that there was nothing weak or soft about her. I zoomed in. The tendons on the woman's arms signified that she was in extraordinary shape. And there was a slight bulge under the cardigan on one side. She was packing heat.

I pressed the intercom button.

"The check's in the mail," I said.

The woman did not smile. I left the intercom open.

"Your downstairs neighbor might live if he gets help right away." She had a slight accent. Nearly undetectable.

I released the button. "Fucking bitch."

In one motion, I grabbed my cell phone and dialed 911.

As I did, I kept my eyes on the screen. The woman's mouth was moving. She pressed the button to open the intercom again.

"...because seconds count, you might want to know where his body is hidden."

"Fuck. You." I said it as slowly as I could.

Behind me, I heard Rosalie's door crack open. I turned. A sliver of Dante's face poked out the open door. It swung open wider. He was holding a baseball bat. Django's snout appeared at knee-height. He gave a loud sniff and then a small whine, sensing the tension in the air.

"911? Where is your emergency?" The voice in my ear startled me.

"There is an intruder in my building," I said and reeled off the address. "The person is outside my front door and claims to have seriously injured one of my tenants. Please send an ambulance right away."

Two people lived downstairs. Chris, who worked a 9-to-5 job, and Jonah. It was probably Jonah, who worked a late shift driving an Uber and would have been coming home right about now.

When the 911 dispatcher reassured me that police and emergency workers were on the way, I hung up. The whole conversation had felt awkward and strained.

I never brought the police into anything. Never.

I'd been betrayed by corrupt cops too many times.

If it wasn't for Rosalie and Dante in the bedroom behind me, I would've opened my heavy steel door and faced the woman. I wasn't afraid of anything she could do to me. If she had a gun, I'd shoot her first. If she had a knife, good luck with that. I was going on my third year of training in Italian *armizare* and *gladiatura moderna*. They were ancient Italian martial arts styles that incorporated daggers and longswords.

The only possible threat I couldn't counter would be if she had an explosive device strapped to her chest and intended to blow us both to Kingdom Come. But her cardigan wasn't *that* thick. The only thing it could possibly be concealing was a handgun.

I knew I could take her, but I held off, instead calling the police.

With her revelation that one of my tenants had been injured at her hands, I'd had no choice.

But I vowed that she would pay for that.

5

Not long after burying his wife, Nico decided to throw a party. The compound was lonely without Sylvia's laughter and the trail of perfume she left behind her in vacant rooms.

He would invite the hoi polloi of Mexico City. The mayor. The police chief. A famous modern artist. His old friend who now ran the Mexico City Zoo. A few other random politicians. Several prominent businessmen. CEOs. Movie stars.

After the party, he would leave the fortress and retreat to his seaside hideaway. It wasn't as heavily guarded, but it was a secret home that only Anthony and the most trusted members of his security detail knew about.

———

Even though there were at least two dozen armed men patrolling the grounds, each guest still was patted down and forced to walk through metal detectors to enter the property. They were led to a pool straight out of Hollywood casting. Nico had been inspired by the pool at Hearst Castle, but he'd adapted it to blend into his country's terrain. The infinity pool seemed to pour off the side of the cliff. It was surrounded on one side by a jungle of wildflowers and tropical plants.

On the opposite side, a massive colonnade rose twenty feet into the sky, giving framed views of the valley where Mexico City lay, miles away.

Beyond the jungle area surrounding the pool was a stone wall and an additional fence— electric—that enclosed five acres of wild terrain and contained one of Nico and Sylvia's most prized possessions. While there were always rumors about what lay beyond the fence and wall, only very special guests saw it with their own eyes.

Tonight's guests would be treated to something even more astonishing.

Waiters in tuxedos circulated, carrying trays of aperitifs and hors d'oeuvres. Music filtered out of speakers throughout the estate and its grounds.

Once everyone had arrived and had a drink in hand, Nico asked them all to be seated in the plush gold and pink chairs scattered around the patio.

Nico stood, facing his guests.

"Thank you for coming. As you know, I am still in mourning for my wife, Sylvia, who was taken from us too soon," he said, looking down. "I have decided that the most fitting way to honor her is to take the money from her life insurance policy and do something that will benefit the children of Mexico City."

People exchanged looks. He saw but did not falter in his speech.

"As you know, our city zoo is in dire need of both renovation and funding."

The head of the zoo, Valeria Flores—an old friend, was sitting in the corner. She nodded, looking surprised. Several other people glanced her way.

"I intend to fix that."

Flores smiled.

"But," Nico continued, "there is something else about the zoo that needs to be fixed. I know that it has struggled to stay afloat over the years. It is exceedingly expensive to feed and house the creatures we have there. Our animal population has dwindled. And yet we are forced to charge the children of our country an exorbitant amount just to come view these remaining specimens." He turned toward Valeria. "This is no fault of yours. I know you have worked hard to keep the zoo open, even sacrificing your own below-standard wages to do so."

The woman nodded, tears clearly visible in her eyes.

"To honor Sylvia, who loved animals more than anything," he said, thinking to himself, *even more than people.* "I have bought the zoo from the city. It will now be free to all residents of Mexico City."

The applause began softly at first, then rose to a crescendo as people stood, clapping heartily.

"Thank you. Please be seated. There is more," he said. He nodded. Men rushed in and set up red velvet ropes separating the stone walkway from the seated guests.

"With the help of our top wildlife experts," Nico said, "we've traveled the world to procure animals that were injured or captured and can no longer live safely in the wild."

The lights dimmed so the backyard was lit only by flickering fairy lights that cast it in a warm glow. The music dropped to a low, soothing murmur of instrumentals.

The crowd fell silent as a man came around the side of the house, dressed in a zookeeper's uniform and leading a white Bengal tiger by a heavy gold leash. People gasped.

A woman dressed the same followed, leading a rare Mexican wolf whose eyes glowed gold as it surveyed the crowd.

Other animals were paraded before the guests, some led by

leashes, others drawn by cages on wheels—a red kangaroo, a miniature sun bear, and a baby giraffe.

In the middle of it all, Nico got a text. It was from Anthony, who was sitting near a large bush of red and purple flowers. He glanced over at the man before reading the text.

"We think we found her. San Francisco. Carmela is on it."

Carmela was one of his top operatives in California. She was ruthless and intelligent and blended into any crowd or any situation.

He sat back in his chair and relaxed, knowing with her on the job, his daughter would soon be home where she belonged.

6

Confident that the police and an ambulance were on their way, I opened up the intercom line again. "What do you want?"

"I mean you no harm."

"You hurt one of my tenants."

"The girl. She is coming with me."

"Fuck you," I repeated, this time with venom in my voice.

But my heart raced. This was about Rosalie. One of my greatest fears was suddenly knocking at my front door.

"She is not yours."

I didn't have an answer for that one. She was mine more than anything else in the whole world had ever been mine. And yet, this stranger was right. She wasn't *really* mine.

"Leave before I take that gun you have under your cardigan and fucking shove it straight down your throat," I said, keeping my voice low and calm.

The woman laughed. "Well, this wasn't exactly how I thought it would go. Let's talk woman to woman. Mother to mother."

"Nothing's stopping you," I said.

"I want this to be as peaceful and easy for the child as possible," she said.

"Well, you shouldn't have fucking hurt my tenant. And you should've called before you showed up at my front door at midnight."

"I wanted to wait until the girl was sleeping. This was the only time I knew for sure we could talk without her listening."

I glared at the woman's face on the screen. She was staring earnestly up at the camera.

"Who are you?" I said.

"I come as an envoy for the child's father. To ask you to make this as easy a process as possible. We don't want the child to be traumatized or feel as if she is forced to come home. The ideal situation is that nobody dies and that she realizes she has your blessing to go to her father's house."

My heart beat double-time. Rosalie's father? The most powerful drug lord in the world, head of Mexico's most deadly cartel, a man whom our government had listed on its Most-Wanted list, had found out that Rosalie was alive.

Icy fear raced through me.

The man was a ruthless killer. Why had he sent an older woman to come knocking on my door, asking nicely for Rosalie? It didn't compute. The woman claimed she wanted to spare Rosalie any trauma. And maybe that was true. But still.

"Why would I give her to you? Why would he want her back now after all these years?"

"If you just open the door, we can talk like civilized people."

"Hey lady, you started it this way, you can finish it this way. The time for civility is long past. That ship has sailed. You fucking hurt, maybe killed, one of my tenants to get into my building. I don't trust you or believe a fucking word you have to say. Get the fuck out before I send a bazooka rocket through that steel door."

I watched her carefully as I spoke. About halfway through my threats, her head turned, and she glanced behind her as if she heard something. I looked at another of the small windows on my computer screen and saw that an ambulance had just pulled up in front of my building. I reached over to unlock the front door of the building remotely. When I glanced back at the window showing the woman, she was kneeling down and placing a small, white piece of paper outside my door. She stood, then turned and ran down the stairs.

I watched as she rushed past the emergency personnel entering the building. One of the young guys gave her a look but then turned back. I punched the intercom button for the lobby about to scream for them to stop her, but as I watched them standing in the lobby, unsure of where to go, I realized my tenant's life was more important right then than stopping that crazy bitch. Besides EMTs were there to help people not stop them. Where were the cops when you needed them?

I flung open my door and reached down for the piece of paper the woman had left, reading it as I raced down the stairs. It had two things written on it:

The first said, "Storage room."

The second was an international phone number.

7

LONG AFTER THE GUESTS HAD LEFT HIS PARTY, NICO STOOD NAKED on his balcony, smoking a cigarette and looking out over the infinity pool. His phone dinged with a text. He looked down. It was from Anthony.

"We have confirmation. It is your daughter. It is only a matter of time now. I will keep you posted."

Nico felt his chest swell with excitement. He wanted to pump his fist in the air. He wanted to pack a bag and leave for America right then. But he knew that it would take time and patience to bring the girl home to him. This was simply step one. But it still brought a wide smile to his face.

"Who is texting you in the middle of the night, *viejo*?" The word meant old man, but the way Valeria used it was also a term of endearment. He wasn't offended. He was only fifty-three, after all. "Should I be jealous, *El Jefe*?" Her voice came from the darkness of his bed where the zookeeper was probably waiting for round two.

"Only if you think I prefer smelly old men like Anthony to you," he said, jumping into bed and reaching for her with a growl.

She squealed in fake fear.

Later, when they both lay in bed staring at the ceiling in the dark, she pulled herself up on her side and lightly traced his lips with her fingertips.

"Is it really true that the girl's mother is the only other woman you were with during your entire marriage?"

"Yes."

He'd told her about Rosalie. It had been tough for him to share the news, and she'd held him so tenderly that he'd wanted to weep.

Now, she kissed his brow before saying, "Wow. So, if I was the last woman you made love to before you married Sylvia, that means you've only made love to three women in fifteen years?"

"Yes. You done asking questions yet, woman?" He reached over and started to caress her inner thigh.

"I guess. I was just worried that making love to you again after all these years would be weird…"

"Was it? Did I lose my moves?"

"Oh hardly," she said, reaching down under the covers until she found what she was looking for. He groaned with pleasure. "In fact, I quite think you've perfected them."

8

I TRIED TO TAMP DOWN MY FURY IN FRONT OF ROSALIE AND Dante, but the reality was that I wanted to strangle that old woman with my bare hands.

That bitch was lucky that Jonah hadn't been seriously hurt. The paramedic said he might have been knocked out by an injection of etorphine. They'd found a syringe on the ground next to him.

Jonah was able to tell me a little bit about it before the ambulance left. He said he'd been unlocking the front door when he'd felt a gun prod his back. He was ordered inside the building and told to unlock the storage room. Once he had, the woman had ordered him to step inside. Then he felt a sting on the back of his neck and didn't remember anything else until the paramedics revived him.

She'd lied. He hadn't been at risk of dying. She'd been trying to scare me. But why?

After the ambulance left, I returned upstairs. Dante was in front of my laptop, which was still open, showing all the building's security cameras.

I quickly filled him in.

"So, he found you."

"And Rosalie."

El Jefe Grande finding out that his daughter was alive had always been a lingering concern. One that I'd consciously—maybe foolishly—chosen not to dwell on for the past two years.

We'd been safe, incognito, for so long. Something had happened. But what?

Hopping online to search *El Jefe*, I saw immediately what it was.

His wife had recently killed herself.

She'd been keeping the secret for years. But what had happened? Was it a deathbed confession?

In reality, it didn't matter. What mattered was keeping one of the most powerful men in the world away from the girl I now considered my own child.

After Dante read the article he stood. "I'm taking her to Calistoga with me right now."

"You think that's safer than here?" I looked around at my fortified loft.

"Only because they know about this place now."

"But still."

"What are you going to do? Stay as a prisoner in your own home while the cartel hunts you? They will kill everyone in your building to gain access. Jesus Christ, Gia, this is the goddamn *cartel*. He will land a squad of helicopters on your roof!"

Dante thought swearing was uncouth, so for him to drop a "goddamn" was serious business.

"Okay, okay. We'll come with you."

"I'll go pack," he said.

"I'll wake Rosalie."

I crept into her darkened room. The ceiling was lit up with a revolving kaleidoscope of the galaxy. The soft sound of rain filtered out through the noise machine on her nightstand.

Before waking her, I crept around and packed her small suitcase with all the things I knew she loved: her favorite clothes, her favorite sweater, a soft lamb I'd bought her for Christmas. After packing, I sat on the edge of her bed.

"Rosalie?" I said, stroking her hair back from her face until her eyes flickered open.

"Gia?" She sat up in alarm.

What else had I expected? Her life had been one of horrible mid-night awakenings.

"We are going to go stay with Dante. As soon as you are in the car, you can go back to sleep. Django will be with you guys, and I'll be behind you in the Jeep, okay?"

"Okay."

I helped her dress and led her to the private elevator that went down to the garage.

I turned to Dante. "Wait for my call. I'll leave the garage first and make sure that bitch doesn't have others staking out the building."

"Surely, she does, though, right?"

I paused. "I don't think so. I think she thought I was some average woman who was raising Rosalie and she could waltz in here and bully me into giving her up."

"That doesn't sound like very intelligent work by the cartel," he said.

"No, but I think that woman is a long way from home. I don't think they had time to research me before she made a move. They were careless and acted rashly. But I also figure this is the last time that will happen. So, you're right, it's time to move now before they rally the troops."

––––––

ONCE I'D LOADED two duffel bags full of weapons and a few clothing items into my Jeep, I scanned the cameras outside the garage door. They showed an empty, quiet street. I flashed my lights at Dante and Rosalie, who were in his Range Rover, and opened the heavy steel garage door. It slid open and I slipped out first, staying parked in front of it until the door closed behind me. I again scanned the street. There were no silhouettes in parked vehicles. I took out my binoculars and glassed all the windows of the surrounding buildings. Nobody peeked out. Then I saw Jimmy, a homeless guy I knew, sitting across the street. He was leaning against a building, tipping back a bottle. I pulled my Jeep over beside him. He jumped up and ran over to my open passenger side window. I reached over and handed him a hundred-dollar bill.

"Hey, buddy. What's cooking?"

"You tell me, Gia."

"Oh, you saw the ambulance?"

"Woke me up."

"There was a woman, an older woman, here. She hurt Jonah and threatened to take Rosalie away from me."

"Wow. That's rough."

"Right?" I said.

"I was sleeping until the sirens." He knew I was going to ask if he'd seen anything.

"What about after?"

"Couldn't get back to sleep. The booms never stop. They keep on coming. I close my eyes and BOOM. They got me. Again. It's Skuli. He just looks at me, and I can't help him, Gia. I can't do nothing."

"Sorry man. I know it's rough. You are a hero. Thank you for your service."

Jimmy was haunted by flashbacks of Iraq. Booms referred to the roadside explosives that had killed his fellow soldiers. It was a damn shame. Every time I said "Thank you for your service," his shoulders went back, and the haze seemed to lift and bring him back to the present. Broke my fucking heart.

"You seen anyone suspicious around tonight, Jimmy?"

"Nope. Except for the sirens and lights. Not a soul. Been quiet. Too quiet, even."

He'd been sleeping when the woman came and went. Too bad. He was my unofficial lookout. My eyes on the street. When he was paying attention, he was good. Damn good.

"Okay, thanks. Take care of yourself. I won't be around for a while. You got my secret number if you need to talk to me, right?"

He put an index finger to his forehead. "Right here. I got it memorized."

"Thanks, Jimmy. Stay safe out here."

I rolled up the window and waited until he settled back down on his stack of cardboard boxes that made up his bed before I texted Dante, who was waiting in the garage for my signal that it was safe.

"Let's roll."

9

NICO WAS UP EARLY. BY THE TIME THE SUN ROSE, HE'D ALREADY reviewed emails and texts from all his top men scattered in major cities around the world. He'd input the sales and expense numbers into reports and then sit back, staring at the numbers that populated before him.

His business was insanely profitable. He had more money than he knew what to do with. He had decided to give the majority of it away. The zoo was just the beginning. He had a lot to make up for. For years, he'd been profiting without giving back enough. Sylvia had often talked him out of his inclination for charitable giving. That was over now.

After Sylvia's passing, his attorney had called him and asked what he wanted to do with the $500,000 Sylvia had been spending each month on designer shoes, clothing, jewelry and expensive month-long trips to Paris, Rio, and Monte Carlo.

"How in God's name did she manage to spend that much each month?" he'd asked, sitting back in shock.

Anthony had cleared his throat. "There may have been some gambling debts involved."

Nico was stunned. "Jesus Christ," he said. "Does she owe money now?"

"Unfortunately, yes."

"Good God."

"Don't worry," Anthony said. "If you like, I can make the transfer from your account and pay off all the debts immediately."

Nico exhaled and closed his eyes, asking, "How much?"

"Four million dollars."

"Do it."

He could afford it. It would make a dent in his bank account, but he had it. He wanted a fresh start. He could not be known as someone who owed money. It would tarnish his reputation.

He'd also ordered Anthony to sell all of Sylvia's belongings, especially her jewelry. All money from that, he said, would be earmarked for a Mexico City charity that helped homeless teenagers.

"Very well," Anthony said.

In addition, Nico ordered that the $500,000 that had been Sylvia's so-called "allowance" should now go to feed starving children in Mexico. The attorney had two days to come back to him with worthy charities in Mexico to be considered.

"One more thing," Nico said. "Do you think this is why Sylvia fired the accountant last month and started doing the work herself?"

Anthony paused for a second and then said, "I suspect this is so."

"Find a new accountant. Bring me three names. I want the financials gone over with a fine-tooth comb. When I make a bid for the avocado holdings company, I want everything to be above board. A legitimate business. Everything must match up and be legitimate. We start fresh from here. I want everything reconciled. Do you understand?

"Yes."

Sipping his second café con leche, Nico used a top-notch secure SAT phone to call one of his men in the jungle overseeing three opioid manufacturing operations along the coast.

As soon as Carlos was on the line, Nico spoke:

"Did you take care of our problem?"

"It is over."

"What did the other men do?"

"They spit on his body."

"Good."

The traitor in question had been siphoning off amounts of the finished product and smuggling it out of the jungle to dealers who were selling it to the Rivas Cartel, the rival drug operation in Mexico. Nico had been trying to ruin the Rivas Cartel, which had gotten out of hand since its leader had ended up in an American prison. Rogue members had started committing some truly heinous crimes. Nico had heard they were targeting children and teenagers for sex trafficking. It was evil. If he could, he would destroy the Rivas Cartel so there was nothing left.

A few weeks ago, Nico had gotten wind of a traitor who was funneling not only money, but information, to the rival cartel.

Anthony had come to him with a pale face and shaking hands to tell him.

"It is Paco Gomez."

"Take care of it."

The plan had been for his head man in the jungle, Carlos, to take out Gomez and his contacts from the rival cartel.

"What about the others?" he asked Carlos now.

"They were strung up in the trees of the jungle. When the courier comes to pick up the shipment tomorrow the message will be clear."

"*Gracias.*"

"*El gusto es mio*" —the pleasure is mine—Carlos said as Nico hung up.

The traitor had been a childhood friend of Nico's cousin's. It was one of the reasons the man had been in a position of power in the operation, where he would actually have enough access to the drugs to steal them. It was a shame he'd decided to misuse that trust and betray Nico.

Despite Nico's cousin's begging, the man had to die. Gomez had to be made an example of what happened to those who tried to steal from Nico Morales.

Nico glanced at his watch. Anthony would be here any second. He straightened his shirt cuffs and stood to pour a second cup of coffee for the attorney, who walked in just in time to be handed the steaming mug.

"I don't have great news," Anthony said, setting his briefcase on the ground beside a chair.

"Let's sit," Nico said.

The older woman had underestimated the situation in San Francisco.

She'd been forced to leave without the girl.

"Rest assured, this is just a minor delay," Anthony said. "Now that we know she is alive and exists, there is nothing that will stop us from bringing her home to you, sir."

"I can't believe that my own daughter was living in San Francisco the entire time. Sylvia told me she was dead."

Anthony gave him a pitying look.

Nico stood. "It's hard to accept that everything Sylvia said is now suspect. It's difficult for me. What if you had found out that everything your wife had told you for fifteen years was a lie?"

"I'd kill her and never feel an ounce of regret."

Nico shot him a look. Sometimes his attorney's cold-blooded attitude was disturbing. Even to Nico, who'd taken his own fair share of lives to get to where he was today.

"What next?" Nico said.

"I've sent Manuel and Lenny to San Francisco to assist."

"I don't want the woman harmed. If she's been raising Rosalie, I don't want to traumatize the child by having the woman murdered." He paused. "At least not in front of her."

"Very well." Anthony stood to leave.

"Please report back with everything you can find."

"I expect to have all that information by this afternoon and hopefully news that we have her in our custody," Anthony said. "Shall we meet at, say, four? For a cocktail and briefing?"

"Very well." Nico said. "Any news on possible accounting candidates?"

Anthony cleared his throat. "We are vetting several right now. The challenge is finding one who is both honest but also willing to turn a blind eye to some of the businesses you are involved in, Nico. It might be a lengthy process."

Nico sighed. He had expected as much.

"Even so—try to expedite this. The attorney for the avocado holdings company is asking for a date to meet, and I don't want to leave her waiting too long."

"These things take time," Anthony said and turned to leave.

After the door to the study shut, Nico stared after the man for a few seconds. Anthony was his most trusted employee and confidant, but then a thought struck Nico. One he'd never had before and one that shook him to the core: Did he even like the man?

Everything he'd once believed was in question now.

Maybe concentrating on Rosalie was exactly what he needed to ground him again.

One thing was certain, being a father was the thing he wanted most in the world right then. It was what got him out of bed each morning.

And now it was so very close.

10

BEFORE I PULLED INTO DANTE'S GARAGE IN CALISTOGA, I CIRCLED the block twice, looking for possible escape routes and traps.

His house was among a few others on a hilly street slightly above the surrounding vineyards. Once I was sure nobody was looking out the dark windows, I pulled my Jeep into the garage. I'd keep it hidden there during my visit.

Dante had known his neighbors for a few years, and they were trustworthy. But he still had no intention of telling them Rosalie and I were hiding at his house. We would keep a low profile and lay low when he went to work at the restaurant each day.

After we pulled in, I got Rosalie settled into bed. Dante turned in as well. I was restless and also didn't feel safe going to sleep. I'd sleep the next day. I needed to remain on guard. At least to make sure nobody had followed us. After that, I would be comfortable leaving Rosalie here for a few days. I would head back to the city where I would hopefully find and confront the Mexican woman. I wasn't sure what would go down when I found her. She'd claimed she didn't want anyone to get hurt. All of this behavior seemed somewhat at odds with the image the media portrayed of *El Jefe Grande*.

Everything I'd read painted him as a ruthless killer.

I had become complacent. I hadn't kept tabs on him for months. I figured that if he hadn't known about Rosalie by then, he would never know. That his wife would keep her word.

With everyone else in the house asleep, I sat on Dante's couch with my feet up on the coffee table, my laptop open in my lap, and a glass of wine at my side. Soft music filtered through his sound system, and the lights were dimmed. I sank into the cushions and sighed. Then I took a sip of wine and started my research.

The number of articles about *El Jefe* was astonishing. His real name was Nico Ortiz Morales, but everyone called him *El Jefe*. He'd gone from being a potentially dangerous contender in the drug war to the DEA's top priority. Holy fuck.

There was a $10 million international reward for his capture and arrest.

The articles I read said he was worth billions of dollars and was extraordinarily intelligent and savvy. He never would've been able to rise to where he now was otherwise.

What had taken the rival cartel leader nearly a lifetime of work had taken *El Jefe* less than five years.

Unlike the other cartel leader, Morales kept a low profile. He wasn't out in Mexico City clearing out fine restaurants so he and his posse could dine. Instead, he remained cloistered in one of his rumored five homes spread across the world. His wife had often traveled and attended events with an army of mercenaries guarding her, but he was rarely seen.

In fact, before the few blurred shots of him at his wife's funeral, the only known photo of him was from five years prior. It was in profile. I studied it. He was an attractive man, at least from what I could see. And he looked older. He had risen in the ranks quickly, but he wasn't a young pup. I wondered what he'd done before taking over the cartel.

I did more digging, reading magazines and newspaper articles, even blog posts. I found that some people viewed *El Jefe* favorably because he gave millions to charity. Others hated him, blaming him for the overdoses and violent drug deaths of loved ones.

One article's headline was *"El Jefe Grande*: Angel or Devil?"

The way I figured it, he probably was a little of both. Sure, he could make those massive donations to help his public image, but I got the feeling he really didn't care what other people thought of him.

Not the man who stayed out of the public's eye as much as possible.

At the same time, he was a criminal who was perpetuating the spread of drugs that ruined millions of lives.

Apparently, he had entire police departments in his employ and his own private SWAT teams. He'd had no qualms about shooting down a DEA helicopter that had ventured near one of his operations the year before. And he was known for executing his enemies or those who betrayed him and leaving their bodies hanging in the jungle to rot.

One Mexican online magazine showed a large picture of three dead men dangling high up in the jungle's canopy after they'd tried to interfere in *El Jefe*'s business.

He was not a nice man.

A tremor of unease ran through me.

I looked up and glanced around Dante's cozy house. I was in the living room, which spanned the length of the house and overlooked miles of rolling hills dotted with vineyards. Besides workers harvesting grapes, the only time Dante saw anyone in the fields below was when a small group toured the winery and adjacent vineyards. Dante's windows were slightly tinted so that even if someone had binoculars, they wouldn't be able to see inside. In the far distance, lights flickered across the miles marking downtown Calistoga.

The only way someone could be watching me was if they were on foot, deep in the vineyards below, and yet I still felt a chill race down my spine.

This ruthless killer I'd been reading about was Rosalie's father.

And he was coming for her.

11

Nico was working out in his private gym when his phone dinged.

Anthony.

"We found them. At a house in Calistoga."

Nico didn't answer right away. He wiped his brow with a towel and stared at his own reflection in the gym's mirrored wall. His face was red. But his shirtless chest looked like that of a man twenty years younger. He didn't work out for vanity's sake, though. He did so to remain strong and fit and healthy for as long as he could.

That was another reason he was extraordinarily disciplined about his alcohol and tobacco use. The cigar the other night was a rarity. He allowed himself to smoke and drink, but in moderation.

Drugs were not even an option. They never had been.

When Nico's first boss in the cartel had held a gun to his head and told him to snort cocaine to prove his loyalty, it had only taken the scrappy young Guatemalan one swift move and a flick of the wrist to disable the man. Five seconds later, he was standing over the boss with one boot pressing down on the man's chest, holding a gun pointed at the man's head.

"How's this for loyalty?" he'd asked.

He hadn't wanted to, but with all the other eyes in the house on him, he knew he had to pull the trigger. He didn't even bother wiping the blood spatter off of himself. He wiped his fingerprints off the gun with his shirt tail, dropped it on the ground, and went to the table to continue playing the card game he'd been engaged in when the cartel soldiers had barged in.

"You have ice in your blood," his cousin had said.

He'd shrugged. It had been his first kill. Nobody else knew that. He'd felt a little nauseous and struggled to hold his cards steady.

Sitting with hooded eyes playing poker, he'd analyzed how the killing had made him feel. Not good. After he'd played two more hands, he'd come to one conclusion: murder was distasteful.

He hadn't felt numb. He'd felt ill. And to be honest, he felt a little afraid. The consequences of his actions might be deadly.

But as soon as he'd refused to snort the cocaine, his fate had been sealed. He would either kill or be killed. But he was a survivor. After humiliating the man by refusing to follow orders, it was a clear choice: he had to kill him then or the man would come back and kill him later.

It was the way of the streets.

That innate understanding was what would save him from poverty. It was what had allowed him to ascend to the highest level of the cartel.

Now, as an adult who was possibly the most powerful man in his country, his killer instinct lay right below the surface of his polished, sophisticated veneer.

Standing and wiping the sweat off his chest, he realized he was lonely and restless.

He'd accomplished everything he'd ever wanted to and with an ease that astounded everyone except him. He was bored with the trappings that would entertain most men: drugs, alcohol, sex, fast cars, big houses, and so on.

While he enjoyed the company of the zookeeper, in reality, their relationship lacked fire. The sex was adequate, but he knew he could go a year without seeing her and not even realize it. She didn't haunt his thoughts the way Sylvia had. When he first saw Sylvia modeling Parisian clothing in a magazine, he had barely been able to sleep until his cousin had tracked her down.

He flew to Paris to woo her, and after just one date where he'd behaved like a perfect gentleman, he'd known he could not die in peace until he'd made her his wife. Except for the one night back in Guatemala where he'd reunited with a childhood love, he'd worshipped Sylvia and honored her. He would never call the night regrettable. But he did acknowledge it was a mistake. He could never regret it, though, because it had made him a father.

As he stepped into the shower adjacent to his gym, he thought about all this and only wished he hadn't hurt Sylvia with his actions that long ago night.

Even though she'd claimed to forgive him, she obviously hadn't, or she would never have kept Rosalie a secret from him.

His anger at her betrayal was tempered by this harsh reality.

But he would let it go.

As he toweled off from his shower, his phone dinged again. Another text. This time just a question mark.

"Same as before. Bring me the child without killing the woman who cares for her."

He hit send.

Even though he knew people feared him too much to disobey his orders, he wondered whether the men who worked for him could manage to do the job without anyone dying.

Well, it was out of his hands.

12

TO KEEP FROM FALLING ASLEEP, I PERIODICALLY STOOD AND CREPT around Dante's house, checking the locks on doors and windows and peeking in on Rosalie's sleeping form. Django lifted his head and wagged his tail in greeting but remained at the foot of her bed, on guard. Good. She was in an interior room with no windows, so that felt at least a little bit safe to me.

In the kitchen, I made an espresso and downed it, carrying a second one around during my patrol. My Glock 43 was stuck in my back waistband, and I had a dagger strapped to my calf.

I was sleepy but felt good. In fact, I'd never felt stronger or more competent in my life. The days of ceaselessly smoking weed and getting shit-faced were long gone.

Even though I felt relatively safe at Dante's, I needed to make sure nobody had followed us.

It was easy to figure out how they'd found us at our loft. Sylvia had confessed her lie to *El Jefe* before her suicide. It had never been a secret that I was raising a child from Guatemala. The lie was that Rosalie was dead and this child was somebody else's. Not *El Jefe's* flesh and blood.

However, the sticking point for me was that he'd sent an old woman to retrieve the girl. From what I knew about the cartel, they shot to kill and asked questions later.

Maybe that had been round one—attempt to bring Rosalie home peacefully. At first. Maybe the stakes were now raised.

As I patrolled the house, I looked for other weapons. When I saw that there was only a set of overpriced knives in my chef friend's kitchen, I went into the hall and retrieved my own bag of weapons.

I'd have to remember to put them all away in the morning once Rosalie was awake, but I decided to plant a weapon at every possible entry point. In the laundry room leading to the attached garage, I stuck a sawed-off shotgun in a hamper of dirty laundry.

At the side door leading to the yard and pool, I tucked an extra *cinquedea* dagger behind a framed picture of Dante and his mother. I put a Ruger LC9 inside a cut crystal bowl on a doily on the same sideboard near a hook for Dante's car keys.

In the hallway leading to the front door, I tucked my AR-15 inside a huge leafy potted plant.

I was pleasantly surprised to find that the house was easier to defend than I might have imagined. The bedrooms were all interior rooms—except for Dante's which soared straight up to make a second story. Like the huge walls of windows facing the rear of the house, someone would have to levitate to gain entry that way. There was a skylight in the great room that led from the kitchen to the living room, but if anybody came crashing through that, I'd have time to shoot them before they regained their footing.

Feeling as if I'd done all I could, I plopped back down on the couch, put my Glock on the cushion beside me, and got back onto my laptop. I was tempted to watch TV, but the sound might distract me from someone trying to break in.

I surfed the web to see if the news had reported on my aunt

lately. Eva was also known as the Queen of Spades. She was known as an Italian Robin Hood trying to stop corrupt Mafia families in Italy who refused to cease their sex trafficking. Her exploits occasionally made international news. When I didn't see anything on her, I went back to hunting for information on *El Jefe*'s past.

I still found nothing that went back very far. I did find a picture of him and his wife at their St. Tropez wedding, but again, his face was in shadows. The man had been very careful over the years to make sure nobody had a decent picture of him. He was no dummy.

I had to admit that part of the reason I wanted to see what he looked like was to see if my beautiful girl had any of his features. Her dark skin, black flashing eyes, thick black eyelashes, and pretty lips were stunning. Strangers sometimes stopped us in the street to comment on her beauty and ask if she was a child model or actress.

She always grew angry at the question.

"I am going to be a scientist. Not a model."

I tried to instill a lack of prejudice and snobbery and told her that there was nothing wrong with modeling. But of course, I also told her of the dangers and the pressure to stay thin and so on.

I could have that type of conversation with Rosalie since she was such a bright kid. She would listen carefully and consider what I said and always come to her own conclusion.

"That's fine for someone else. But I don't care about being rich. I want to make a difference in the world. Find a cure. Help sick people. Do something that matters."

Damn, girl. While my heart swelled with pride, I also couldn't help but wonder if this all stemmed from the atrocities she'd seen in her young life.

Young people around her had died from preventable

diseases in her Guatemalan town. Others had been murdered over drug deals. Some died just because they disagreed with a person with a gun.

I hadn't realized I'd drifted off until a slightly muffled thud sent me off the couch to a standing position with my Glock clutched in both hands. I froze, listening for what had woken me. I watched as the front door handle turned. At the same time, I heard the slightest sound of movement to my right, from behind the door leading to the garage. Someone was at the front door. And someone was in the garage.

I stood between both, uncertain which way to go.

13

BECAUSE I WANTED THE AR-15, I DECIDED TO HEAD TOWARD THE front door first. I'd taken two steps in that direction when the front door splintered open in a burst of gunfire. At the same time, Dante flew out of his room and raced into Rosalie's. Her door slammed behind him but not before I got a glimpse of a shotgun in his arms.

He wasn't a fighter. But I knew he wouldn't hesitate to shoot anyone who came through that bedroom door. Near the front door, I scooped up the AR-15 from the potted plant and began firing toward the door. At the same time, I heard muffled gunfire from the kitchen. After several bursts to ensure I'd scared anyone away from entering that way, I raced back to the kitchen in time to see a man step through the splintered remains of the door there and raise the muzzle of a shotgun toward me. I dropped to the ground and rolled around the corner just as he fired. Plaster fragments from the corner of the wall between us rained down on my head.

Doing an Army crawl, I peered around the corner, using a small end table against the wall as cover. I could see legs through the opening at the bottom of the table. I lifted the AR-15 and fired, aiming for the knees. The figure dropped instantly, firing off another round that went into the ceiling and sent another rain of debris down on the floor. As soon as I saw the man hit the floor, I squeezed off a round at his head. I was still lying down when I saw another figure step through the shattered remains of the door to the garage. Still partially hidden by the end table, I decided that the last trick worked so well, I'd try it again. I aimed for the dude's knees. He fell to the ground in a heap. Blood was spurting in a frenzied arc onto the wall of the kitchen. I'd struck a femoral artery. I put a bullet in his face to make sure he wouldn't be coming after me from behind. I backed up around the corner, heart pounding, adrenaline spiked to an all-time high. I sat there, shaking uncontrollably and staring at the door leading to Rosalie's room.

Dante knew not to make a sound, and I'm sure he'd instructed Rosalie to do the same.

He knew to wait for me to tell him it was safe. He also knew that if he waited a long time and it was quiet and he hadn't heard from me, that it had gone south.

The roar of the guns had temporarily deafened me to any sound except the ringing of my ears. I waited, eyes darting in each direction and straining to hear, but when the ringing stopped and I hadn't been attacked again, I stood.

I set the AR-15 down on the end table. I had to go get Rosalie and Dante, and we had to get the hell out of there before they sent more people. That was the only thought I had in my head: Get them, and get the fuck out.

I'd stepped out of the cover of the wall toward the bedroom when I heard a sound that made me freeze. Someone else was in the house.

Out of my peripheral vision, I saw the older woman standing there, both arms extended as she pointed a serious-looking gun at me.

"You are only alive because *El Jefe* has ordered it so," she said.

That made me pause. I turned my head to fully face her.

"But if I have to kill you, I will tell him it was unavoidable. You've made that easier for me by killing Manuel and Lenny. It is justification enough to take your life."

"Then why don't you do it?"

"Because believe it or not, I agree with *El Jefe* that your death would further traumatize the girl. She is all I care about. Not you," she said and spit on the kitchen floor.

So, *El Jefe* was worried about traumatizing Rosalie? He should've fucking thought about that before he sent his goon squad into Dante's house.

"Where is she?" the woman said.

I stared at her. She was fucking crazy if she thought I was going to answer.

"I don't want to waste time searching the house. Call the girl out now."

Instead of answering, I glared at her. I prayed that Django wouldn't bark or do anything to indicate where they were hiding.

Before I could react, she'd sprinted toward me and raised her arm to hit me in the head with her gun. I was able to raise my arm to fend her off, and the blow smashed down on my forearm instead, nearly sending me to my knees. Skinny bitch was stronger than she seemed.

As I crouched in pain, I reached down and grasped the dagger strapped to my thigh. I kept it pressed against my leg, keeping my body angled so it was out of view.

As I rose, I caught a blur of silver and black as she swung the butt of the gun. It struck me across the face. The blow spun me and sent me reeling. My teeth stung, and I tasted the metallic sweetness of blood in my mouth. I used the momentum of my spin to come back around with the dagger raised in my right hand. I whirled and slipped the dagger's blade into the base of her neck near her hairline. She crumpled immediately. I stood, panting, and wiped away a stream of blood dribbling from my mouth. I saw the gun near her right hand. I kicked it, and it skittered across the kitchen floor. She still didn't move.

I was afraid to leave her there to rise like Freddy Fucking Krueger to kill me. But I also was too wary to reach down to check her pulse. I could imagine her plunging some hidden knife into my eye if I got close enough.

I kicked her. Nothing. I shoved her over with my foot. Her head flopped loosely from side to side. Her wide eyes stared at nothing. I nudged her again, softer this time. Her head lolled to one side. A trail of blood dribbled from her mouth, and I finally decided she was truly dead.

I barely made it to the kitchen trash can before I vomited until I dry heaved. I heard a scuffling sound in the bedroom and Django whining.

"Give me a minute," I called through my spittle.

I wiped my face and headed toward the bedroom door.

"Dante?"

"Gia?"

"We need to leave," I said. "But Rosalie needs to be blindfolded or something."

"Okay."

Panic swelled in my gut. I looked around at the bloody massacre around me.

"We need to go now!" I screamed, but the door remained locked under my palm.

"Just moving stuff I used to blockade the door." Dante's voice was shaky.

He opened the door. A bed mattress and frame was upended, and furniture was helter-skelter. Rosalie stood before me in her nightie with Dante's black T-shirt tied around her face. He was bare chested, wearing only pajama pants. His eyes widened in horror as he saw the scene behind me.

"Your poor house. I'm so damn sorry," I said.

He closed his eyes for a second and then exhaled.

"Let's go."

We raced to the garage with Django at our heels. The garage door was wide open. We put Rosalie into the backseat of my Jeep.

"You can take off the shirt now, sweetie," Dante said.

She was trembling slightly. She hadn't spoken a word since the bedroom door had opened, revealing her standing there. It freaked me the fuck out.

Blocking our way was a shiny, new Dodge Ram.

"Dante, I've got an idea."

Twenty minutes later we were going down the road. I was in the Dodge with three dead bodies flopping around beside me. Every time I took a corner a little too sharply, the bodies shifted. I screamed every time the old woman's arm touched mine. But if we kept the bodies inside Dante's house there would be too many questions.

I had already destroyed his life enough as it was.

But sitting in a truck with three dead bodies was the stuff of fucking nightmares.

It was way worse than carrying the bodies from the house and hoisting them into the truck. Rosalie had been instructed to close her eyes the entire time. I'd checked and she was leaning against a window with her eyes closed. She was a good girl. She was feisty and rebellious in all the right ways but knew to listen when we were serious. Unlike other kids her age who thought it was funny to disobey their parents, in Rosalie's short life, she had learned that listening to those she trusted could mean the difference between life and death.

It took us about forty minutes to get to the spot. It was still dark, so the road leading up to the rocky outcrop overlooking the Pacific was deserted. I took the Dodge off-road as far as I could before I hopped out. There was enough of an incline that if I put the truck in neutral and then pushed it, it would roll off the cliff. I did so but couldn't get the truck to budge. I looked over at Dante. He hopped out and, between the two of us, we were able to start the truck rolling.

We waited to get into my Jeep until we saw the truck reach the edge of the cliff and then tumble down the rocks until it landed in the water and began to sink. It floated for a few minutes and then submerged. I'd cracked the windows to let the water into the cab.

It wasn't until we were on the freeway heading south that I spoke again. I'd been watching Rosalie's head in the rearview mirror for a few miles. She kept falling asleep and jerking back awake. Django had his head on her lap and was softly snoring. When her head had finally lolled to one side and her mouth dropped open in deep sleep, I spoke.

"I don't know where to go now," I said, hating the whine in my voice. "Your house...Your beautiful house, Dante."

"It's just stuff. That can be replaced."

"But I brought those psychos there. It's my fault."

"Gia, we're famiglia. Maybe not by blood, but in every other way. This is what family does. Nothing matters except that the three of us got out of there alive."

"Where will you go? What will you do?"

"We'll figure all that out."

"What about your restaurant?"

"Lars can handle it. I already texted him that some crazy people were after me and that I had to go into hiding. He has power of attorney. He can handle anything while I'm away."

"Maybe we should turn around and head for Canada," I said. "Get out of the country or something."

"I have a better idea," Dante said.

"Pray tell?"

"We *should* leave the country. But let's go the other way."

Mexico.

"You're joking, right?"

"Serious as a heart attack. Where else would be the least likely place for us to hide?"

I frowned. "Right in the belly of the beast?"

"Damn right. But maybe not the belly, maybe just a limb. Like the left arm."

"Baja? As soon as we crossed the border, we'd be sitting ducks," I said. "They'd take Rosalie and kill me and you before we made it to Tijuana."

As soon as I said that, I quickly glanced in the rearview mirror. Rosalie was still asleep, thank God.

"Didn't you say that Eva has a place in Cabo?"

"Yes."

"Okay. Here's the plan..."

Dante's plan made sense. Somewhat. We'd stop by my friend Darling's salon to grab some fake passports she'd made for us a while ago. Darling's hair salon was her baby, but she made the big money in providing false documents to people eager to escape desperate situations. That usually meant women escaping abuse. A few weeks ago, she'd told me she had made fake documents for me, Rosalie, Dante, and a few other of our friends. Just in case.

We'd also leave Django with her. That dog loved her.

Then we'd fly to Cabo San Lucas. We would fly separately. Me alone. Dante with Rosalie—his "daughter." We'd meet at Eva's condo. *If* we could reach her and get her permission.

The plan involved a lot of moving pieces, but it might work.

"Let's start making some calls," I said. "I'll start with Eva."

I had kept her black business card embossed with a spade in

my wallet near my driver's license since she'd first left it for me. The other side had nothing but a phone number printed in raised red letters the color of blood.

She picked up immediately.

"Gia?"

"I need your help."

14

NICO WAS HAVING A HARD TIME GETTING BACK TO SLEEP. HE'D fallen into a deep slumber right after an epic lovemaking session with Valeria but then startled awake about a half hour before. He should've heard from his crew in California already. He checked his phone again. Nothing.

Valeria stirred beside him, making a soft mewling sound like a kitten.

He frowned. He hadn't intended for her to stay the night. He didn't feel that intimately about her. He respected her and enjoyed her company—and her body—but he'd been with the same woman for fifteen years. He wasn't ready to commit or settle down. He'd told her just that tonight and she'd simply smiled and said, "Oh, honey, I'm too old and settled in my ways to want more than just this."

And yet, here she was in his bed, snuggling up to him in the night.

He'd have to insist they take a short break. Her actions belied her words, and he didn't want her to get hurt. Besides, the more she was around and the more she knew about his business, the more vulnerable they both were.

She had a full, busy life away from him.

If his enemies found out he cared about her, she would become an easy target. Her work at the zoo made her vulnerable to all sorts of attacks—unlike him in his secluded enclave.

At least with Sylvia, he'd been able to send armed guards to escort her wherever her many exploits took her. Once, even that had almost not been enough. She'd been on the beach in Rio when a *loco* member of the Rivas Cartel had come screaming out of the waves wearing a snorkeling mask and wielding a huge knife. He'd charged Sylvia, shouting something about revenge and had made it within a foot of her before one of the guards had stopped him with a bullet between his eyes.

Extracting Sylvia and his men out of the country without a big scandal or police investigation had been a clusterfuck of international payoffs and negotiations.

Finally, at dawn, Nico dialed one of his men in California.

"We've lost contact." The voice was wobbly. This man, a newer soldier in the cartel, probably thought Nico would punish him for it. Nico waited for the man to continue. "I have a man on his way to the location as we speak. I should hear back within the hour."

Two hours later, while he and Valeria were in the middle of round two, his phone dinged. Fifteen minutes later, he reached over to his phone.

"Mission failed. Soldiers KIA."

At the same time, his phone rang. It was Anthony.

"The truck is pinging in the waters of the Pacific. We could try to retrieve it, but—"

"I don't care about them. Where is the girl?"

Silence.

Nico closed his eyes in frustration.

Valeria reached over and stroked the top of his hand.

He resisted the urge to jerk his hand away. If anything, he

prided himself on his ability to remain cool and collected under pressure.

Only those who were weak reacted with anger or frustration. Powerful men like himself had fierce control over all emotions and acted accordingly.

His eyes snapped open.

His words were calm when he spoke next.

"Call me when you find the girl."

He hung up without waiting for an answer.

"Everything okay?" Valeria asked.

He kissed her brow.

"Let's go eat breakfast."

15

THIRTY MINUTES AFTER LANDING IN CABO, MY DRIVER PULLED INTO a gated compound in the rolling hills above the Cabo San Lucas marina.

Tall, steel gates led to a paved driveway and a windowless and doorless expanse of stucco that reared up three stories.

"Follow the footpath to the entrance," he said. "The door is unlocked. There is a sheet inside with all the information you will need, including my phone number. I live nearby, so feel free to call if you need anything whatsoever."

"Thank you," I said. I waited until he'd slipped out the small door to the side of the gate before I started toward the paved path that led around the side of the house. It was lined with tropical plants. A three-story high stucco wall was to my right and the house was to my left. As I rounded a corner, the path opened up to a backyard with a pool. The house was lined with windows on this side and the back.

The Mexican sun was strong, and the shimmering turquoise water in the pool beckoned. I saw Rosalie leaning down and swirling her tiny hand in the water. She and Dante had arrived just before me.

"Hey!" I said. "Why don't we go see if we can find something to swim in and come back out. Maybe with snacks? Who's hungry?"

"Me!" Dante said, coming outside the house.

Rosalie jumped up and grinned. I was relieved to see she was back to her normal self, seemingly taking in last night's events with aplomb.

The inside of the house was simple but cozy and comfortable. Sleek lines and neutral-colored furniture paired with brilliantly colored paintings on the wall and an abundance of tropical plants. There were four bedrooms upstairs. One was clearly the master bedroom where Eva stayed. A massive bed with a black leather headboard and stark white comforter dominated the room. There was little else inside.

Rosalie and I took a guest room with two twin beds. The bedspreads were a weave of bright pinks, turquoises, oranges, and greens. A colorful, framed print of Frida Kahlo took up one wall, and Mexican rag dolls in colorful dresses sat center stage on the low wardrobe. Rosalie started to play with them immediately, making them talk to each other.

Dante took the room beside ours. It was outfitted with a queen bed with a bright red coverlet and small, Mexican tile mirrors covering one wall.

"Gia?" it was Rosalie. "What do I swim in?"

I frowned. I could wear my black bra and panties and be fine, but I worried Rosalie would be self-conscious swimming in anything less than an actual bathing suit.

I opened the closet doors and smiled. Eva had thought of everything.

There were five colorful sundresses in Rosalie's size. The closet also contained two pairs of jeans in my size and two gray long-sleeve T-shirts like those I favored.

A pair of Adidas in my size were also on the floor of the closet along with some ballet flats for Rosalie.

"Look in the dresser drawers," I said.

Almost immediately, Rosalie exclaimed. "There are two bathing suits that I think are my size!"

She was so excited I couldn't help but smile.

"And a black one for you!"

There was a knock on the door.

Dante stood there in red swim trunks.

"Who wants to learn how to do a cannonball?"

"Me!" Rosalie said.

"Go get dressed!" I said, pointing at the attached bathroom. "We'll meet you downstairs."

I wanted a few minutes alone with Dante downstairs.

I hadn't told him the exact details yet, but my plan was for him to basically be Rosalie's nanny here at Eva's house while I went after her father.

16

I WAS DOZING IN A LOUNGE CHAIR BY THE POOL, SOOTHED BY THE sounds of Dante and Rosalie splashing in the water beside me—giggles, shouts, and squeals of delight creating the most blessed soundtrack I could imagine.

For the first time, it struck me that in all senses of the word, I was a mother.

And it felt good. Better than good. It felt amazing.

Suddenly the world grew silent, and I sat up and opened my eyes, alarmed.

That's when I saw her. She was standing at the point where the paved path opened up from between the house and wall to the backyard.

Eva. My aunt. The Queen of Spades.

Rosalie had sidled up to Dante at the side of the pool, eyes trained on the woman in black. Eva always had that effect. No matter how many times she appeared, the power she effortlessly exuded took everyone's breath away.

She wasn't a large woman. Maybe 5 feet, 7 inches or so. She had long, flowing black hair, always dressed in black leggings and a tight, long-sleeve black T-shirt, and it was rare to see her without the huge black sunglasses she was wearing.

She pushed those back onto her head and smiled.

It was as if the tension broke, and Rosalie squealed in recognition, all wariness and apprehension gone.

"Eva!"

She pulled herself out of the pool and rushed over to my aunt, wrapping her arms around Eva's waist and pressing her little wet body to Eva's. My aunt's smile was megawatt as she looked down. Then she crouched down to Rosalie's level.

"*Cariño!*"

Rosalie excitedly spoke to her in Spanish, telling her about how much she liked the room and the dresses and the swimsuits.

"I have more fun things planned," Eva said, straightening. She reached for Rosalie's hand. "Do you want me to show you the game room? We have video games. Do you know how to play? And chess. And cards."

"Yes, please. I love poker!"

"So I've heard," Eva said. "Let's go. And then you can help me figure out some other fun toys to buy for your vacation here."

Eva winked at me. She and Rosalie held hands as they went into the house, not caring that Rosalie's wet body dripped water all over the floor in a trail behind them. Dante tsked and followed behind with a towel, crouching to wipe it up.

I laughed. So like him.

———

LATER, after a dinner of fish tacos with heaps of fresh salsa and guacamole, Dante tucked Rosalie into bed.

He came down and sighed. "She misses Django."

"I'm sure."

"I'll arrange to fly him down," Eva said.

"He's with Darling. So he's in good hands."

"I know. But if it brings her comfort to have him here, I'll arrange it," Eva said. "Plus, while this place is safe, it wouldn't hurt to have an extra level of protection."

"That's what I need to talk to you about," I said.

In the end, in addition to bringing Django down, Eva arranged to have two armed guards at the house at all times. If Dante and Rosalie wanted to go into town, they could, as long as the guards were with them.

"Good. I'm sure Rosalie will love the beach."

"I think we are okay here," Eva said. "She will not stand out. Dante, your skin is dark enough for you to be easily mistaken as Mexican. You can still pretend to be her father. Tell her to call you Papa in public."

"Sounds good," Dante said.

I glanced over at him, hearing something in his voice. I wondered if he and Matt had planned on adopting after they'd married. Did he want to be a father? For some odd reason, it was something that had never come up between us since we'd lost Matt and Bobby.

Dante would be a terrific father. No doubt.

He excused himself to go to the bathroom. I turned to Eva, who leaned over and refilled my wine. I noticed she was still sipping her first glass.

"Eva? If something happens to me, I want to make sure Rosalie is taken care of."

She didn't answer. She just met my eyes and nodded solemnly.

"Can you help me make arrangements for Dante to be her father? Legally. Officially. All of that. I think she needs a dad."

Eva looked down. Something crossed her face that I didn't understand. It looked like a flash of pain, but just as soon as I saw it, she glanced back up and smiled. "That is a wonderful idea, Gia."

That's when it struck me. I hadn't even considered her to be the one to take care of Rosalie.

"Oh my God. I'm sorry. Would you? Could you? I mean, I guess I didn't even think..." It all sounded lame. I tried again. "I just know you are so busy and travel so much and are basically training an army..."

She reached over and put her hand on mine. "Gia. It's okay."

We sat there for a few seconds in silence, then Dante came back in.

"What?" He said looking from one of us to the other.

"Dante, would you—if something ever happened to me—would you take care of Rosalie?"

For some stupid reason, my heart was pounding.

"Of course. Without question. I told you, Gia, we're family. I'm her uncle after all."

I smiled. Of course he was. And Eva was her aunt.

I turned to Eva. "That girl is so lucky to have an aunt and uncle like you guys in her life."

Eva smiled at my words, but there was still the slightest sadness beneath. There was so very much about her I didn't know. And might never know. I was still astonished every time she entered my life, swooping in like an avenging angel and then disappearing again into her mysterious, Italian world.

"I have to go back to Italy tomorrow," Eva said, as if she'd read my mind.

"I need your help finding him," I said. Panic soared through me at the thought of her leaving.

"I know. I've done some research. I have the location of his main residence high above Mexico City to the north of the capital. It is heavily fortified. Like a fortress."

"Hmm."

"He spends the majority of his time there. But as luck would have it, I heard he might be going to his beach house this weekend near Cuixmala."

"And?"

"He thinks it is a secret. He will be less guarded."

"Then that's where I'll go. Where is it?"

"Between Puerto Vallarta and Acapulco, in a 30,000-acre biosphere reserve."

"Sounds nice," I said.

"What will you do?" She didn't seem concerned, just genuinely curious.

"I'll try to reason with him at first."

Eva nodded, not taking her eyes off of mine. "And if he won't listen to reason?"

"Then I guess I'll have to convince him."

"I can arrange to have you on a flight to the mainland tomorrow afternoon unless it's too soon. But I think if you can beat him to the location of the beach house and establish yourself as a tourist in one of the nearby hotels it will be a better cover story if you are caught," Eva said.

"I don't plan on getting caught."

"So tomorrow then?"

"Yes," I said. "The sooner the better."

17

HE HAD WAITED LONG ENOUGH.

It was time.

Everything was in place.

The inquiries were a definite concern and at first had thrown him for a loop, but as was his way, he'd immediately pivoted, shifted gears, and come up with a solution that was not only viable but an even better plan than the original.

He wondered why he hadn't thought of it immediately.

As soon as it had come to him, he'd known exactly how to handle all of it. The only difference was that this plan had a ticking time bomb.

But that made it even more exciting.

Soon, though, it would all be over. He could slip away and live like a king for the rest of his life.

Nobody would know any differently.

They would assume he'd been murdered as well.

18

A SERVICE WORKER'S VAN WOULD TRANSPORT NICO TO HIS BEACH house under the cover of darkness. Inside, it was fitted with reclining leather seats and a full bar, which he only used for the seltzer water and healthy snacks.

Anthony would be staying in Mexico City in an attempt to clean up the mess from the high-profile murders in the jungle. In hindsight, Nico wished he had given explicit directions to keep the slayings low profile. Instead, to send a message to the rival cartel, the bodies had been hung up above a sign that everyone could see. Journalists had easily gotten hold of the gruesome photographs and spread them across the Internet. The murders had made international news. Leaders from around the world were calling "*El Jefe Grande*" a barbarian.

It was indefensible, but part of him had still wanted to issue a statement that the bodies of the men were those of rival cartel members. These were not innocent farmers, as some had said. Every man hanging from the fence was a cold-blooded killer and drug cartel member. But there was no opportunity to defend himself.

Anthony said he would stay back and do damage control but

insisted that Nico make himself scarce for at least a week, if not longer.

It was a good time for him to hide out at the beach house. He needed to keep a low profile while the international crowd put pressure on the Mexican president to go after him.

"Will Valeria be accompanying you?" Anthony had asked.

"No." He said it matter-of-factly, and Anthony didn't raise an eyebrow. In fact, he seemed pleased. The greedy son-of-a-bitch didn't like anyone in Nico's life who might play a more important role than he did. Sylvia was the exception. His disdain had been barely disguised.

Nico didn't say he was looking forward to going to the beach house as a way to force a break between him and Valeria. She was busy getting the renovated zoo up and running with the new animals, so he thought it would be a good time to physically separate himself from her beguiling body. The sex was good, but not great, mainly because there was no true tenderness there. At least on his part. He couldn't help but see her as a platonic partner. He liked her fine. But as he had for years—as a friend. And frankly, that wasn't fair to either one of them. Not at their age. At least not unless she felt the same, which she clearly didn't. He could tell she was developing feelings for him by the way she looked at him. He had to cut it off before it was too late and she got hurt.

19

IT TOOK ME A FEW HOURS TO GET FROM MEXICO CITY TO THE remote seaside village.

I'd kept my carry-on bag tucked under the plane seat in front of me, sweating bullets. Even though I'd traveled with it numerous times, I always imagined I'd get caught with its contents and be thrown in prison for life.

It was a specially designed bag that made my guns and knives invisible to X-Rays. I wasn't sure exactly how it worked, which was part of the reason I was always worried it would fail. The secret compartments were lined with some magical material or something.

But I was always a nervous wreck until I'd cleared security at airports. I tried to play it cool while acting like a spoiled heiress to dispel any suspicion. It wasn't a tough acting job since I'd been exactly that not so long ago.

The village north of Cuixmala was called Farallon, which sounded like home to me since we had the gorgeous wild Farallon Islands in San Francisco—a national wildlife refuge home to birds, seals, sharks, whales, and a crazy scary number of mice. The Mexican Farallon was surprisingly free of American tourists and tourist shops. When my car pulled into the small main street near the beach, there was a café, a restaurant, a small market, and two gorgeous one-story resorts with rooms that opened up to the beach and ocean beyond.

The hotel across the street from mine was nicer, but mine was right on the beach. I would forego room service, maid service, and a heated pool for a back door that opened up to the beach.

My room was tiny but clean. I immediately walked straight through the room to the sliding glass doors and threw them open to the sea breeze. Then I unearthed a bottle of whiskey and a pack of English cigarettes I'd bought duty-free at the airport and settled in at the small café table on my beachfront patio.

It had been more than a year since I'd been this alone. My entire life for so long had been caring for Rosalie. I had left most of my vices behind during that time. But, now, I'd decided I'd treat my two days of waiting for *El Jefe* as a mini vacation.

I would read at least three of the five books I'd plucked from Eva's library and drink whiskey, smoke cigarettes, and nap in the sun until my skin turned bronze.

Then, on the third day, when *El Jefe* was expected, I'd get to work. Figure out a way to meet him and then—*bam!* —surprise him by telling him who I was and what I was there for: to ask him nicely to back the fuck off. Or kill him. I was prepared to do that if it meant saving Rosalie from him.

In case he could recognize me on sight, I'd brought thick stage makeup to disguise my scar, huge black sunglasses, a big floppy hat and bright orange, pink, and turquoise dresses that San Francisco Gia wouldn't be caught dead wearing. But more than that, I intended to spread a story around town before he arrived that I was a rich divorcée from Palm Beach, Florida, licking my wounds—and looking for love.

After a quick nap, I dressed in the pink dress with gold high heels and dark sunglasses that covered the upper third of my face and headed for the one restaurant in town.

"Patio please," I said in Spanish when the hostess greeted me.

The hostess brought me chips and salsa, which I eagerly dug into until the waiter came.

"A bottle of your finest Champagne," I said with a smile.

"Are we celebrating something *senorita*?"

"Yes. I'm celebrating a divorce from my cheating, son-of-a-bitch husband. And there was no prenup, so right now I'm here to spend all his money, drink as much as I want, and maybe find a handsome Mexican man to spend some time with."

I figured I'd put it all out there immediately. The waiter didn't blink.

Instead he made an eloquent bow. "I can help you with the first two, but I apologize for the third, I am of no use. My wife would not approve." His eyes twinkled.

I laughed loudly and with delight. This was going to be fun.

"I, unlike my cheating husband, respect marriage vows—my own and others—so we will get along just great, Mr...?"

"You can call me Miguel."

"Thank you, Miguel. I'm Serena," I said, using the name from the fake identification documents Darling had prepared for us in San Francisco.

"Of course you are," he said. "What can I bring you *Senorita* Serena?"

"Please bring me your favorite dish. And something strong to drink in addition to the Champagne. My husband didn't drink, so I have a lot to make up for in the drinking department."

He raised one eyebrow. "You are staying at the El Dolfin?"

"Yes."

"I will be happy to serve you. But be careful. There is a group of American men here who are leaving tomorrow. They are bad news. I would not want you to drink so much you didn't have your wits about you. I do not trust them. In fact, I would recommend my busboy, Sam, escort you back to your room. At least for tonight."

"Do you really think that's necessary?"

Miguel's face grew somber. "I cannot say for certain, but there is some talk that maybe a local woman was mistreated by them."

I tried to keep my face neutral. It took a supreme effort, and I swallowed and gathered myself before responding.

"I appreciate the warning. Can you tell me? Are they at the same hotel?"

"No, the one across the street."

"Thank you. I will either leave early or I will take your kindly offer and ask for an escort from Sam."

He left to get my drinks, and I counted to ten to gather my wits.

Every fiber of my body wanted to go back to my room, get my dagger, find the assholes, and slice their balls off. *Mistreated*? I would bet anything they'd raped the woman.

It would, however, be best for me to keep my eyes on my mission. I would eat quickly and then retreat to my room for the night. In the morning, the men would hopefully be on their way out of this peaceful town. And safe from me.

But just as Miguel brought me Champagne and a shrimp appetizer, a group of three loud American men walked out onto the patio. Everything about them disrupted the peaceful evening. The sun had just set, and the beach before me was bathed in a warm glow that matched the one in my belly from the alcohol. The men sat nearby and were laughing and speaking loudly about some fishing trip they'd been on earlier in the day. I was grateful for the large, dark sunglasses that hid my eyes as I studied them. They all wore wedding rings.

I was not facing them directly but could tell right away when they zoomed in on me: Woman. Alone.

The low murmuring of their voices sent a zing of alarm through me. I wasn't afraid of them, but I didn't need a confrontation to blow my cover.

They stopped talking, and I could feel their eyes on me.

The sexual innuendos reached me easily. They weren't trying to keep me from hearing. They were trying to intimidate me. It made my skin crawl, and I was a killer. How must it feel to be an innocent normal woman and have those predators eyeing you and whispering like that? It filled me with fury.

Do. Not. Blow. Your. Cover. Santella.

I would ask for the check and leave before I went over there and kicked the biggest one in the teeth with my stiletto.

Then one of them began singing that 1980s or 90s song, "I Wear My Sunglasses at Night." And one of them said, "With my big titties hanging out."

I stood, my chair scraping back loudly, and rushed into the restaurant. Their laughter rang in my ears as I stepped inside.

Miguel looked at me and shook his head. I handed him a fistful of pesos and headed for the door.

"Do you want me to find Sam?"

I paused, my hand on the doorknob. I was going to refuse, but not for the reason he thought. I didn't want Sam around if the men followed me. I didn't want any witnesses to what I was going to do. But it would also seem odd if I refused an escort.

"I'm going straight back to my room and barricading my door. They just ordered another round of drinks. I don't think they will leave until those come. Will you delay the drinks slightly to give me time to get back?"

"*Claro.*" Of course.

I turned to leave.

"*Senorita*? You gave me too much," Miguel said before I made it to the door.

"That local woman?" I asked.

"Yes?"

"Is she okay?"

He nodded solemnly.

"What is her name?"

"Catalina."

I pressed my lips together and walked out.

20

While still at his Mexico City home preparing to leave, Nico had received a phone call: something strange was going on in Farallon.

Three drunken American tourists had raped Catalina, a local woman whom he'd known for years. When he found out the men were scheduled to leave soon, Nico decided to send some men ahead of him.

"Make it hurt," he said. "And make sure before they take their last breath they know it is because of what they did to Catalina. In fact, invite her to watch. Or participate if she likes. If she wants to cut off their manhood, give her the tools. Let her run the show. Or let her have nothing to do with it. It's up to her. And when it is over, dispose of the bodies and all the men's belongings. Prepare the townspeople for inquiries from American authorities. The cover story is that they rented a small boat one morning and never came back."

When he was satisfied the men would pay for what they did to Catalina, he hung up.

Valeria was watching him.

"You don't mess around, do you?" she said lightly.

"These men raped a friend of mine."

She nodded. He couldn't tell if she approved or thought he was despicable.

He sighed.

"What is it?" She was suddenly in front of him, looking up into his eyes.

"That phone call is why I need to have this conversation with you," he said.

"Oh, it's over now?"

"You just heard. You know my life. You cannot be a part of it. You are an innocent."

"But Sylvia could?"

"She was not innocent like you."

"I'm not innocent, Nico." Her words were calm.

"But you are not damaged," he said. "And I want to keep you that way."

It was true, but it was also easier than telling her he didn't love her. Enough time had passed that any potential love would have blossomed by now. You couldn't force things like that.

"I knew this was temporary," she said. "That's why I tried really hard not to care."

He waited. Her eyes pooled with tears.

"*Mi cara*," he said in a soft voice.

"Don't," she said and turned away. "It's better I know now."

She picked up her bag and walked out without looking back.

He felt a pang of guilt and sadness but, at the same time, he felt a small sense of buoyancy. The relationship had brought an intimacy he craved and needed but also a small burden of guilt since he did not love her. It was good that it was over. For both of them.

21

ONCE OUTSIDE THE RESTAURANT, I SLIPPED OFF MY HIGH-HEELED sandals and walked as fast as I could without attracting attention. Nobody was out in the sleepy village. I listened for any sounds and turned to look frequently behind me to make sure nobody was following. I made it to my hotel without being trailed.

In my room, I immediately changed into jeans, sneakers, and a T-shirt. I tied my hair back and tugged on a baseball cap. I strapped on my custom-fit holster and tucked my Glock, with its suppressor attached, inside.

I crossed the street quickly, keeping to the shadows. The men's hotel had only five rooms situated in a semi-circle around a swimming pool.

It didn't take me long to find their rooms, all in a row. They'd left all the lights blaring and the curtains open. The remaining rooms were also unoccupied.

I broke into the first room easily by picking the lock with the tool kit I'd grabbed from my suitcase. Once inside each room, I rummaged around until I found passports and airplane tickets. I did this in each room. I set the documents aside and then proceeded to clear their rooms of all personal belongings by dropping them quietly into the pool. I wasn't sure if the manager stayed at the hotel, but I didn't want to attract any attention if I could help it.

I wanted to teach them a lesson they wouldn't soon forget. I realized I was trembling with rage. The most important thing was to not blow my cover. But at the same time, I could not sit by and let this sort of behavior take place.

Tell their wives they're going on a fishing trip to Mexico and then come and rape the local women? It was disgusting.

In fact, what I was planning to do was letting them off easily. What I really wanted to do was cut off their dicks and stuff them down their throats. But I had to be cautious.

I left all three doors wide open and sat in a lounge chair by the pool with my gun resting on my lap and my nerves on fire. I made two phone calls from my cell phone, managing to convey my desires in rusty Spanish, and then I sat back to wait.

The men didn't return until much later. I could hear them coming a half block away. I lit a cigarette as they drew near. They were talking about trying to find me and have a last "fling" before they left.

I waited until they saw the open doors to their rooms. They turned and clocked that all of their belongings were either bobbing in the swimming pool or had sunk to the bottom.

"Jesus Christ!" one of them said.

"You said 'fling.'" I spoke in a low voice from my seat in the shadows. "Is that what you call raping a woman? A fling? Is that how you justify it to yourselves? To each other? To your daughters, maybe?"

The men's heads swung in unison to where I sat behind them.

"What the fuck?" A tall skinny guy said.

I took a long drag of my cigarette.

"Do you think the Mexican authorities will take kindly to you raping one of their women?"

"Who the fuck are you?" another one said.

"I'm here to teach you a lesson," I said, exhaling my cigarette smoke.

"Oh yeah?" The biggest one started stumbling my way.

I raised my gun. "Easy sailor."

He drew up short.

"Fuck, she's got a gun."

"It has a silencer," I helpfully pointed out.

"What do you want from us?"

"I really want to kill you, but I don't think I can do that right now."

"*Right now*?" I could see the man's Adam's apple bob.

"Strip," I said.

"What?"

"Take off all your clothes."

"No fucking way."

I was up and had the gun shoved halfway up the guy's nose before he could react.

"I said strip."

"Okay," he said.

I stepped back out of range of any wild throws or kicks he might attempt.

He took off his shirt first. I could see the rage race through him as he did.

He kicked off his shoes and dropped his pants to the cement,

The other two followed suit meekly.

"Stand there. Together."

While I wished I had time to do more, I settled for taking

their cell phones and snapping pictures of them all standing naked in a huddle and then sending them to the wives' phone numbers. They were easy to find. They were the most frequent numbers dialed or in the "favorites."

I sent a text that said. "I am a pig and a rapist and don't deserve you. You should ask me what I did to Catalina in Mexico and take me for every cent."

"What are you doing with our phones?"

I didn't look up and just continued texting as I spoke. "Did you know her name was Catalina?"

One of them swore softly. Another moaned and said, "I told you that was a bad idea."

"If it was a bad idea, why'd you go along with it, fuckhead?" I asked.

He shook his head. "Please, please let us go. I've been sick ever since it happened."

"Not so sick that you didn't talk about doing the same thing to me tonight, though, right?"

He closed his eyes. *Good. Be afraid.*

I started to walk away with their phones

"Wait!" the tall skinny one said. "You can't just take our phones."

"The hell I can't. There's a car out front. It will take you to the airport. You will remain there for the rest of your trip and wait for your flight. Pick up your clothes and go now. You can dress in the car. It is leaving in exactly two minutes."

"Fuck you."

I didn't know who said it. I paused, and without turning said, "A car has already gone ahead to the airport. Your passports and plane tickets will be waiting for you at the airport's lost and found. If you don't get in the car and leave immediately, I will make sure that the passports never make it to lost and found. If you are late, they will be destroyed."

"Shit."

I heard them scrambling to grab their clothes as I dipped into a corner corridor that led to the alley. There, I crept around the building and peered out from the side until I saw all three pile into the car and it drove away.

22

NICO WOKE LATE AT HIS BEACH HOUSE. THE SUN WAS HIGH overhead. He hadn't arrived until late the night before and hadn't turned in until almost dawn. He'd been up late thinking about his life and wishing that he had fallen in love with Valeria. He was lonely.

But all that would end when his daughter was there with him.

Anthony had said they were following leads. He told Nico not to worry. He was confident they would find the girl before Nico left the beach house.

And Nico believed him. Anthony was utterly reliable. When he said something would happen, it did.

Nico climbed out of bed and was preparing to do his morning workout when he saw he'd missed a call. It was from Anthony.

He dialed his attorney's number.

"Your men arrived at the hotel," Anthony said. "But the American men were already gone. They went to the airport."

He glanced at the clock. "Are they still in the country? Were they warned?"

"Interestingly enough, there was somebody else in town unhappy with their actions."

Nico froze. Who would dare to act without his orders in Farallon? It was his town. From top to bottom. From north to south.

"Do you remember that woman they said arrived a few days ago?" Anthony said.

"The Palm Beach divorcée?"

"Yes."

"What does she have to do with it?"

"Maybe everything."

23

IT WAS NEARLY TOO GOOD TO BE TRUE. ALL HIS PROBLEMS MIGHT be solved in the simplest manner. And sometimes simple was best. Just like *ex parsimoniae*, also called "the law of briefness," specified: "more things should not be used than are necessary."

24

THE NEXT MORNING AT BREAKFAST, MIGUEL BROUGHT ME COFFEE and then paused.

"Good morning," I said.

"*Senorita*, you do not need to worry anymore," he said.

"Oh really?" I looked up, sounding curious.

"The American men are gone."

I made an exaggerated sigh and leaned back in my seat. "Oh, thank God."

There was not even the slightest suspicion in Miguel's eyes as he smiled at my reaction.

"It is good, no?"

"Yes," I said, exhaling loudly again. "I was actually considering hiding in my room all day until I knew the coast was clear."

He nodded seriously. And then he leaned down conspiratorially. "Somebody took care of them."

I gasped. "Are they dead?"

I could've won a fucking Oscar for the whole performance.

He shook his head. "No, but they were forced to leave last

night. All of their belongings were destroyed. Thrown in the pool."

I sat up straight. "Good."

"Yes," he was practically gleeful.

I leaned over and whispered. "Who did it?"

He kept his voice low. "I cannot say, but I do know that we are expecting a very powerful, important visitor today. He has sent his men ahead of him. Maybe they learned of these men and wanted them gone ahead of time."

"Oh," I made my voice sound intrigued. "Is it a famous movie star or celebrity I might know?"

"I cannot say, *senorita*. My apologies."

It was time to change the subject.

"Thank you for that wonderful news. I think I will celebrate by having a mimosa."

He raised an eyebrow.

"You know—orange juice and Champagne."

"Aha. Yes. I do know that. Mimosa. That is good. I might even have one myself," he said with a small laugh.

Once he'd left, I finally relaxed. My cover remained intact.

And I'd just received good intel—*El Jefe* was arriving today. Not tomorrow as expected.

After a quick breakfast—an egg dish with chorizo and cheese—I downed my mimosa and coffee and, with a cup of coffee to go, headed back to my room. It was time to scope out *El Jefe*'s place from the beach.

Eva had said it was south of the downtown area and had tall concrete walls separating it from the beach.

I changed into a red bikini, put a white crocheted cover-up over it, slathered my scar with stage makeup, donned my dark sunglasses and floppy hat, and packed a straw beach bag with a towel, a book, suntan oil, and a bottle of water before setting off.

But at the door, I turned and stuck one of my daggers into the bottom of the bag. Just in case.

About a quarter-mile down the beach, the houses became larger—big white stucco or sandstone homes with floor-to-ceiling windows facing the ocean. Most had low brick walls separating their backyards, filled with lounge chairs, from the beachfront.

All the houses had signs advertising alarm systems. Most looked empty. It must have been the off-season.

Even from a distance, I could tell I was growing close to *El Jefe*'s beach house. A few of the homes now had large walls, but this one was over the top. Inside its walls, it was surrounded by a forest of palm trees and other tropical foliage. I idly walked out to the water, stepping in the wet sand with the waves lapping my feet, so I could get a better vantage point of the house beyond the wall.

As I drew closer, I only got a glimpse of the uppermost story of the house. It rose slightly above the canopy of trees. It looked like a glass-walled penthouse with a small deck. Since I was still some ways away, I was staring directly at the home and practically jumped when I saw a figure standing on the upper deck. Slowly, in an attempt to not draw attention to myself, I slightly shifted my head so it was more forward facing, but kept my eyes—behind my dark sunglasses—trained on the figure. *Shit. El Jefe* was already there.

This was the big boss in the flesh. A jolt of fear and excitement-spiked adrenaline ripped through me as I realized I was looking at *El Jefe* himself. He wore a white button down shirt and loose white pants. He was leaning against the low railing of the upper deck and staring out at the sea. His head turned to clock my approach. I kept my gaze straight ahead, as if he could see through my sunglasses, and watched him out of my peripheral vision as I passed along the beachfront in front of him.

I'd planned on possibly spreading out my towel near his house and sunbathing that day, but now it seemed obvious and contrived to do so since I knew he was already there.

I could practically feel his eyes on me as I continued down the beach. I went about another twenty minutes down the beach until I hit a rocky outcrop where that stretch of beach ended.

I walked leisurely back toward the house one more time, this time pausing briefly before I reached it to extract a bottle of water from my bag and take a long pull on it. I wasn't directly in front of the house, but I wasn't far away, which gave me a chance to stop my stroll and watch the house out of the corner of my eye. It looked deserted now. The upper deck was empty. But I'd definitely gotten his attention earlier. My hope was that he'd send someone to town to ask about me. And good old Miguel would tell him the story about the Palm Beach divorcée, heart-broken but looking for help in healing her heart with a hand-some Mexican man.

Right before I tucked the water back into my bag I caught a glimpse of someone standing at the upper deck window looking out. At me.

I straightened and moved on, passing by the house and keeping my eyes on the stretch of beach before me.

Back in my room, I slammed and locked the door behind me for some reason. I lay on the bed; my heart was pounding. And it wasn't from the walk. Game time, bitches.

I closed my eyes and tried to remember the man standing on the upper deck in detail. I was pretty far away, but I recalled an image of a man with a full head of slicked-back black and gray hair and a matching goatee. Dark skin was a stark contrast to his white clothing. But his posture leaning against the rail was what interested me most. He appeared confident, secure, poised. Powerful.

My eyes snapped open, and I laughed at myself. All that from a few seconds of glimpsing the man? What? Absurd.

I sat up and reached for my to-go cup of coffee. It was cold. I went down the hall to the ice machine and made it an iced coffee.

Then I grabbed my woven bag and stepped outside onto my tiny patio. A foldable lounge chair rested on the wall. I picked it up and headed down to the water. About halfway to the waves, I set up my chair. I rubbed my body down with the suntan oil—the coconut, tropical smell taking me right back to summers at Carmel Beach with my girlfriends as we worked on our tans. I was always dark by the end of the first day. My fair-skinned friends acted jealous, but there was always that underlying hint of prejudice.

Even on the Monterey Peninsula where the Italians were the most powerful businessmen—the ones who founded Cannery Row and still ruled that stretch of coast—people looked down on Italians.

A lot of it I didn't comprehend at the time, but now as an adult, all the looks and the strange comments from my friend's parents— "Your dad seems to do very well in business? Isn't he friends with the Bonadonna family?"—made sense now.

They all thought they were better than us. That much had always been clear to me.

The first time I realized it as a kid was when a classmate had called me and my father a racial slur.

Thank God those days were gone.

I wouldn't trade all the money in the world to be a teenage girl again. Pure. Fucking. Torture.

Sipping on my coffee, I fished my cigarette pack out of my bag. I would quit again as soon as I was back in California, I vowed. I needed something to tamp down this surge of anxiety I felt. It was like the adrenaline rush I used to feel before a martial arts sparring match in high school. It was the anticipation of battle, confrontation, something big.

I lit the cigarette and had just exhaled when I heard the sound of a boat approaching. Soon, there was a larger size ski boat straight out in front of me on the water. It only had one person in it—the driver. *El Jefe*. I watched as he dropped anchor off the side. I leaned forward in my chair, fascinated. What in the fuckity fuck was going on? He'd blatantly stopped right in front of my hotel.

He was fiddling around with something, then he stood and stripped off his shirt. Even from my seat I could see he was in excellent shape. Then he dropped the loose white pants, revealing swim trunks that looked like spandex bicycle shorts. He stepped onto the sleek bow of the boat and walked confidently to the pointy prow. He'd seemed to not notice me. Until now. He turned to look right at me.

My breath caught in my throat. He gave the slightest nod and then executed a perfect dive off the boat and sliced into the turquoise waters.

I quickly gathered up my things and hurried back to my patio. There, in the safety of the patio's shade, I lit another cigarette and watched him paddle around the perimeter of the boat until his sleek head emerged out of the water at the stern. He pulled himself up by a small ladder. I watched as he stood in the center of the rocking vessel and dried his hair with a white towel. He pulled up the anchor and started his engine, heading north, away from his home.

I realized I'd been standing there with my mouth wide open as my cigarette had burned down to the filter, a huge, long ash plopping to the ground.

Well. Well. Well. He'd certainly done a good job getting *my* attention.

Mission accomplished, sailor.

Thank you, Miguel, for spreading word about the distraught Florida divorcée looking for love. Good thing old *El Jefe* was apparently a player. This would be easier than I thought.

OF COURSE, HE KNEW WHO SHE WAS BEFORE SHE WALKED BY ON the beach below his house while trying so hard to seem nonchalant, thinking foolishly that sunglasses and a hat could fool him. He'd studied pictures of her over the past week. He knew every curve of that body. How her jawline was defined. The pout of her lips. That sexy scar near her temple.

As soon as he'd learned that a woman had confronted the American rapists, he'd known. Reports of a black-haired beauty who could take down three large men at once made it pretty obvious. Although, interestingly enough, she'd allowed them to live. Unlike the fate of his three soldiers in Calistoga. He was intrigued.

It was obvious it was the same woman.

Giada Valentina Santella.

AFTER *EL JEFE*'S PERFORMANCE AT THE BEACH THAT AFTERNOON, I knew he would be at the restaurant that night for dinner. What I hadn't anticipated is that he would already be there seated at my "usual" table.

As Miguel walked me in and I saw *El Jefe* sitting there, I drew up short.

He stood and smiled. "Would you care to join me?"

I purposefully hesitated for just a second and then gave a slightly surprised and uncertain smile before nodding.

He jumped up and pulled out my chair for me. When I looked around, Miguel had disappeared.

I demurely unfolded my napkin and placed it in my lap, trying to avoid his eyes.

When I looked up, he was staring. He had flashing black eyes and was unexpectedly handsome. I hadn't heard this about him. He exuded a powerful animal magnetism that made me wary.

I waited for him to speak first.

"I don't usually encounter visitors like you in my secret hideaway," he finally said. He frowned as he said it. *Fuck*. He was suspicious.

"Who said this is 'your secret hideaway?'" I said lightly. "Do you own this town?"

He let out a loud laugh. "No."

I raised an eyebrow.

"It's just that it's not on the regular tourist destination path. Especially for Americans."

I lifted my glass of water to my lips and took a sip before answering. "Which is precisely why I'm here."

"So I've heard," he said in a murmur. "A beautiful woman named Serena who obviously has a fool for an ex-husband."

"I guess nothing remains secret in this town," I said. I kept my tone light and my manner nonchalant.

"I make it my business to know what's going on."

"What is your business?"

He smiled and his teeth flashed white. "Knowing what's going on."

"The advantage is yours," I said. "I don't even know your name."

He leaned back, grinning.

"I see how it is. That's okay. I can get all the dirt on you from Miguel," I said.

He laughed. "If anyone knows my secrets, it's Miguel."

"Really?" I smiled and then picked up the menu.

It was silent for a few seconds before I looked at him over the menu. "Do you always go swimming in front of the Dolfin?"

"Never."

"Oh, I see," I said in a matter-of-fact voice.

There was a commotion by the front door. I looked over. Three men in black stood there. With one glance I knew they were armed. My heart jumped into my throat. They were on to me. *El Jefe* knew who I was.

Seeing my alarm, *El Jefe* gave me a curious look.

"Don't be afraid. They are with me."

I exhaled loudly. "Oh. Okay. I think."

He stood. "Excuse me."

Standing in the doorway, he and the men spoke in low voices. He kept glancing over at me, making my dread rise.

Were they telling him who I really was? Was this it?

Then he walked back to me.

"I'm sorry," he said. "Something urgent has come up."

And without another word, he walked out.

I stared after him for a few seconds. The three men followed on his heels without glancing back at me.

Soon Miguel was at my side, asking to take my order.

Despite my joking earlier, Miguel ended up being a truly terrible source. As I ate my seafood dinner alone, he refused to answer any questions about *El Jefe*.

"Can you at least tell me his name?"

"*Senorita* Serena, I would move heaven and earth for you, but this I cannot do."

I frowned. What kind of chokehold did *El Jefe* have on this man? On this whole town?

Nico's men had managed to intercept the American men in the parking lot of the airport, but someone had seen them, and it would take several phone calls and wire transfers to important Mexican officials to make sure the men had "never been seen" entering Mexico City.

It was unfortunate he had to handle that right then because he'd just had the pleasure of meeting Gia Santella. Her beauty was raw, sensual, like a black panther. He found he was reluctant to part with her company. But business was business. And he knew where she was staying.

He couldn't wait to find out why she was here.

She obviously didn't have his daughter with her.

He could only assume one thing: she was here to kill him.

Her recklessness was refreshing. She had no idea what she was up against. He wasn't sure if he wanted to kill her or kiss her. But that was not important. After all, he was *El Jefe Grande*. He could do both.

WHEN *EL JEFE* WALKED OUT OF THE RESTAURANT, LEAVING ME sitting there alone, I was at a loss. It took me a few seconds to readjust my plans.

I decided to take my time eating, ordering *sopes*, topped with refried beans, *carnitas,* and *queso fresco.*

Running out after him would set off alarms. He obviously had this whole town in his pocket. I should just assume that there were eyes everywhere.

As much as I wanted action, my best bet was to play the bored divorcée. I'd set up camp on the beach again and read my book while working on my tan.

After I paid Miguel, I left by the beach side of the restaurant, slipping off my sandals to walk on the sand. I would take the same way as I had the day before, passing by *El Jefe*'s house. For all he knew, I took this morning walk every day, right? And it would help burn off some of the excess adrenaline I was feeling from being so close to him.

When I neared his house, I could tell there was nobody on the upper deck. I passed and the house seemed deserted. I walked again to the end of the beach before turning around.

There was no sign of life at the beach house when I passed it a second time.

Back at my hotel, I set up the lounge chair again and cracked my book, hoping the sound of a ski boat would approach again. But the water before me remained empty.

I only left the beach to restock on food, cigarettes and drinks, or use the bathroom. I finished my book and started another. I spent the day eating, napping, and reading.

At one point, I looked down at my skin—I was now at least four shades darker than I'd been when I first arrived in town; thank you Italian DNA—and decided I needed to set up the beach umbrella that was propped in a corner on my patio.

I couldn't remember the last time I'd spent an entire day doing practically nothing. It felt amazing, but by the time the sun was growing low on the horizon I was bored.

Inside my room, I showered with the bathroom door open, alert to any sounds from the rest of the room. After my shower, I dressed in a white sundress that made my skin seem even darker, grabbed my bag, and headed for the restaurant as the sun dipped down to the west.

It was Friday night, so a few of the tables at the restaurant were already occupied. One table held a small family. Another had three couples who looked about my age. The women wore dresses and high-heeled sandals. A third table had an older couple holding hands. No sign of *El Jefe*.

"This is when our small town comes to life," Miguel said as he seated me. "Our population doubles and sometimes triples on the weekends. We are a weekend getaway for those who live in the big city."

"Not very many tourists, huh?"

"No," he said, pouring me a glass of red wine. "It is rare we have American tourists. We are a bit of a secret. Not a big tourist destination. That is why it was so surprising to have the three men and you all in one week."

"That is odd," I said.

"Please tell me if this is none of my business, but why do you hide your beautiful eyes behind dark sunglasses?"

I smiled. "How do you know they are beautiful?"

"It is impossible they are not," he said. "Forgive me for asking."

His face colored.

At first, I'd thought *El Jefe* had put him up to the question, but as he blushed, I realized he was genuinely curious. I felt guilty for lying to such a nice guy, but it was necessary.

"No apology necessary," I said. "I'm happy to explain. I suffer from epilepsy. Bright lights can trigger it. Even at night. I've worn them so long I don't even think about it anymore."

"I don't know why I was so rude. Please forgive me." He bowed.

"Nonsense," I said. "Nothing to forgive."

"If you say."

He waited for me to order.

"Miguel, would you order for me tonight? I would be grateful if you would pick out a meal that you enjoy."

He smiled. "Of course. I know just the thing."

He began to walk away but paused when I spoke.

"One more thing," I said and waited until he turned so I could read his face. "Did you ever find out what happened to those American men? Why they left early?"

His face remained expressionless. "No idea, *senorita*."

I smiled. "Thank you."

Miguel brought me an outstanding but simple dinner comprised of fresh seafood—shrimp, mussels, and scallops, lightly cooked in a mint sauce that tasted like springtime in each bite. He brought a white wine to go with it.

I ate slowly, waiting for *El Jefe* to arrive. Soon, the other tables emptied and refilled with new diners, but there was no sign of the drug lord. It was becoming awkward for me to be there for so long, so I asked for the check.

"This was perfect," I said to Miguel as I stood to leave. He had scooted back my chair for me, so when I turned to face him, we were face to face. "Miguel, the handsome man who joined me the other day. I haven't seen him since. I'd like to invite him to go snorkeling. Are you sure you can't tell me his name? Or how I can reach him?"

"Hopefully you will meet up with him again during your visit. You make a striking couple," Miguel said, skillfully avoiding answering my question.

His eyes were twinkling as he said it. Damn. But for some reason, his response reassured me that maybe *El Jefe* didn't yet know who I was and hadn't told everyone in town that I was a dead woman.

29

As much as he wanted to go to the restaurant or even go knock on Gia Santella's door, Nico holed up in his house and spent the day working out, reading his new favorite book, *Aztec* by Gary Jennings, and napping.

He wanted her to come to him.

That way, if he did need to kill her, it would not take place in public.

After all, she *was* an American citizen.

He owned the town—he practically owned the entire country of Mexico—but he also knew that money talked. And that Gia Santella had plenty of it. He'd also heard rumors that she had an aunt, an Italian woman, who could be extremely dangerous to him if Santella's death were traced back to him.

For all those reasons, he would be cautious. While it would be easy to have his men storm her hotel room and kidnap her or even kill her and dispose of her body, he wanted to hear what she had to say first. Maybe she was going to ask him for a ransom for Rosalie. Maybe she would try to kill him. He laughed at the thought. Whatever her plan was, he would wait for her to come to him.

But after a day spent waiting, Nico grew impatient—a weakness of his—and came up with a plan.

30

WHEN I WOKE UP AND WAS STRETCHING BY THE SIDE OF MY BED, I froze.

A white envelope had been slipped under my door in the night.

I used my dagger's blade to slit the top open. A small hand-written card was inside.

"Please join me for dinner. 8 p.m." It was signed, "Nico Morales."

His real name.

I didn't know what to think of that.

But I sure as hell was going. I had a thigh holster that could fit my gun under a full skirted sundress. The dress was red and backless and flared out from my waist, dropping to my knees. I tried on the holster with the gun in it and the dress over it.

I patted myself down in the front. Unless he grabbed my thigh, I didn't think he would feel it. I didn't *think*. That really wasn't good enough. I looked again in the mirror. *Fuck*. It did bulge out slightly at one leg. I switched it with the thigh holster for my dagger. That worked better. I'd have to tuck my Glock into my handbag and keep it nearby.

Even though I was wearing my dark sunglasses, I lined my eyes thickly with black kohl and used extra stage makeup for my scar.

It felt like war paint. It felt necessary.

I did some stretches in my room, but didn't feel prepared. I hadn't trained for a few days and wanted to warm up. I snuck down the hall and found what I was looking for in a small utility closet. Back in my room, I twisted off the head of the mop and practiced some of the grappling moves and swordplay that I'd been studying for the past two years.

At eight, I stepped out of my room and headed toward the front desk to ask about hiring a cab or driver. I was going to be late on purpose. If it took forty-five minutes for a cab or driver to get here, so be it. I don't think the big boss ever had to wait. I was going to show him from the start that I called some of the shots here—that I wasn't intimidated by who he was and the power he wielded. At least that was my plan. I pushed back the small doubt that was creeping in, attempting to erode my bravado. I had to walk in there like I was his equal, or he would never take me seriously.

But when I entered the lobby, there was a man dressed in an ill-fitting gray suit over a white T-shirt. He had short hair and looked like he'd done time. When he saw me, he nodded and gestured toward the front door. Through the windows, I saw the black car in the driveway.

I hesitated, but only for a second. If *El Jefe* knew who I was, getting in that car was the same as signing my own death warrant. I had to take the chance. Because if he knew who I was, refusing to get into the car wouldn't save me.

31

HE PACED THE UPPER DECK, WAITING FOR HIS CELL TO DING THAT she was on her way.

It wasn't the first time a woman had tried to toy with him by being late. It didn't bother him. His anxiety stemmed from worry that she wasn't coming at all.

He'd dismissed his staff for the night. After the driver dropped her off, they would be alone. It was extremely rare that he was ever completely alone.

His lifestyle and his occupation meant that having armed guards nearby at all times was absolutely necessary. He knew his behavior tonight was risky. Anthony had scolded him, telling him he was a fool.

"You don't know who has gotten to her," Anthony had said. "And even if you are confident you could take her down, she took down three of your soldiers. Or, what if she is not the actual threat? She could be a decoy. Or, what if word spread to the Rivas Cartel that you were unguarded tonight, and they've sent a hit squad to take you out? I do not approve of any of this."

"I understand and respect that," Nico had said. "But it is my life. If I can't make decisions such as this, then I am a prisoner of my own making, now, aren't I?"

It was true, but also a nice way to tell Anthony to back off and mind his own business.

If the head of the world's most powerful cartel couldn't make his own decisions, then what was it all worth?

He hadn't risen to the position of power he was in by being foolish. Once Gia Santella was inside, he would lock down his house with his top-of-the-line security system. If anyone attempted to gain entry, he would know.

The stars were brilliant in the sky that night. He leaned on the rail of the upper deck and wondered what Gia Santella was going to say to him. She was an exciting woman. Something about her was so raw and animalistic. He was, frankly, used to polished, sophisticated women. This woman was primal. She had a careless nonchalance about her. She truly didn't care what anyone thought of her. At the same time, she was like a coiled snake, exuding danger and suspense. And, good God, did she have the balls of a matador to come here to Mexico to find him. Some would call it stupidity, but he knew it was fearlessness.

He'd thought a lot about her the past two days. He'd never met anyone like her.

The anticipation of having her in his house was building. But he stayed motionless, staring out at the star-filled night. In the distance, the waves lapped against the beach in a soothing rhythm. His phone dinged.

"She is on her way."

All his big plans to make her wait downstairs and to remain aloof went out the door. He took the stairs two at a time.

When the car pulled up, he was waiting outside.

32

THE DRIVER DIDN'T SAY A WORD DURING THE SHORT DRIVE OVER TO *El Jefe's* house. Even though he'd given me his name in the invitation—Nico Ortiz Morales—I had a hard time not thinking of him by the name the media had given him.

I had the ominous feeling I was being driven to my death and was overcome with the sudden urge to text those I loved one last time to tell them how I felt.

Sorrow swept over me as I realized the list of those I would text was woefully short. Rosalie. Dante. Eva. Darling. My sensei, Kato.

But I brushed that sadness aside. I was goddamn lucky to have that many people I loved in my life. As an orphan, I'd created my own family.

And each person in it was like a brilliant gem set in a priceless ring. Golem's "Precious" had nothing on my bling.

I didn't need to send them a last text for them to know how I felt. I made sure to live every moment fully and never part on a cross word. I'd been estranged from Dante before, and I'd vowed it would never happen again. If I had to camp out on his front stoop for the rest of my life begging him to reconcile, I would do it. Life was too short to let misunderstandings separate me from those I loved and who loved me.

That's why I was here. To fight for Rosalie. So we would not be separated. Because I loved her. But more than that, she needed me.

This monster, as charming as he was, was a fucking drug lord. What kind of life would that be for a little girl?

A small part of me wondered at that assessment of him. I had to remind myself that most people in supreme positions of power like *El Jefe* had gotten there through a combination of irresistible charm and deadly drive. Right then, all I'd seen was the charm. However, he was a murderer. Point blank.

The car pulled into his driveway. He stood near the front door with his hands in his pants pockets. When the driver opened my door, *El Jefe* greeted me with a huge smile.

Fuck. It totally threw me off.

What *was* his deal?

————

As soon as we were in the house, he turned and set what looked like an elaborate alarm system. When he turned back he said, "Unfortunately, to some people I'm more valuable dead than alive. I'd hate to have some of those people interrupt our dinner."

"Or making sure I don't leave?"

He laughed but then turned to me. "The code is #4467#."

I eyed the contraption.

Of course, he could be lying. But I didn't think so.

"This way, Gia," he said, gesturing toward the interior of the house. "I need a sous chef for my dinner plans. You good with a knife? Oh, wait, of course you are."

He walked away, leaving me standing there speechless.

He fucking knew who I was.

I gave the alarm system one last glance before I followed him down the hall toward a brightly lit kitchen.

33

WHEN I STEPPED INTO THE KITCHEN, I SAW A GRANITE ISLAND covered in stacks of vegetables: tomatoes, avocados, onions, garlic, jalapeños. There were several bowls and knives on the counter. A cutting board off to one side had some type of thinly sliced meat on it.

"Do you like guacamole?" he asked. He'd tied a blue flowered apron on.

I stood inches away from the huge butcher knife on the black granite. He had his back to me at the stove, pouring some oil into a deep skillet. It would take less than five seconds to snatch the knife and throw it into his back. I'd gotten pretty damn good at throwing knives at a target. I rarely missed.

But *El Jefe* didn't even look my way as he shook some red pepper flakes into the oil. The kitchen was starting to smell fragrant. I was frozen, half afraid and half exhilarated that he knew who I was. He turned to get the meat off the counter. I watched as he lifted the cutting board and lay the slices of meat in the oil one by one.

"My mama made the best salsa in Guatemala. It is a closely guarded secret. Only other *famiglia* are allowed to know all the ingredients. You and I are, in a way, connected through Rosalie, so we are somewhat like family. Because of that, I think it is fair that you are privy to the recipe. Plus, I have really been craving it lately. I have a fresh bag of chips from the café that are still warm and salty. We will have that as our appetizer."

Still, I stood without speaking or moving. I needed to gather my wits. And fast. I was afraid to speak. I didn't want to say something stupid or have him hear any fear or uncertainty in my voice.

I took a few seconds to gather my thoughts and then reached over to grab a yellow flowered apron that was flung over the back of a chair. I tied it on and then picked up the butcher knife.

"Okay, sailor," I said. "I assume I chop the tomatoes first?"

He looked over his shoulder and clocked me holding the gleaming butcher knife in one hand. I smiled and cocked my head.

"Yes, please. The tomatoes are washed and ready to go. There are two dozen. I think we must use them all. At least enough to fill that stainless-steel bowl." He paused, taking me in. "I should've let you wear the blue apron. Yellow is not your color."

Fuck you. But I bit my tongue and swallowed down the words.

"But the blue looks so good on you," I said instead. "Does your army of assassins know that blue aprons with flowers on them bring out your eyes?" I asked.

"My white butcher's apron is in the laundry," he said and winked. "Besides, I was kidding about the yellow. You look stunning."

I ignored the compliment and set to work on the tomatoes using a small marble cutting board.

"*¡Buen dios!*" he said loudly, and I jumped. "I can't believe I forgot the music. One cannot cook without music."

"Agreed," I said. "I was going to say something..."

He laughed. I liked his laugh. A lot. He leaned over and hit a button and some up-tempo Latin music filtered out of speakers above us. He hummed and danced a little as he flipped the meat with tongs. I watched him from behind as I chopped. Could this be any more surreal? No. No fucking way it could get any stranger. I was standing in the kitchen of the world's top drug lord, chopping tomatoes and watching him dance in front of a stove with a flowered apron on. *What the fuckity fuck*?

When the tomatoes were done, I reached for the jalapeños. He glanced over and when he saw me slicing the jalapeños, he rushed over.

"No, *mia cara*, you need gloves."

"Huh?"

"You are Italian, no?"

"Um, yeah. Italian-American." I squinted as he reached into a drawer and extracted some latex gloves.

"We Latinos know that you must use gloves with peppers. Wear these. The seeds and juices from those particular peppers are known to cause third-degree burns. The capsaicin is very strong. That is why I only have two small peppers for that entire bowl of salsa."

He took one of my hands and slipped the glove on, working the latex onto my hand with both of his hands in a caressing motion. When I looked up, he wasn't looking at my hands but was staring at my face. I swallowed.

When he reached for my other hand, I plucked the glove from him.

"I got it," I said in a matter-of-fact voice. "I think you need to check the meat."

His head swiveled. "Oh, yes." He was at the stove shaking the pan with the meat in it before I could blink.

"Thank goodness. This is a tricky part," he said. "The meat

has to be just right or the whole meal is ruined."

As I finely minced the onion and garlic, he extracted the strips of meat from the skillet with tongs and set them on a plate nearby. Then he poured more oil and red wine into the skillet and the liquids began to boil.

He came over and grabbed a handful of the onion I had just chopped and dumped it in the skillet where it instantly sizzled. He plucked a massive bouquet of cilantro from a glass of water and chopped the leaves and stems into smaller bits. He tossed some into my bowl of salsa ingredients and then some into the skillet with the onions. Then he added the meat back into the skillet, turned the heat down and put a lid on it.

"Aha. Now, we have a celebratory drink as the meat soaks up the juices and the salsa marinates."

He poured wine into a blue glass and handed it to me.

"Shall we?" He gestured to the back door. I followed him out to a small patio area with a fire pit and Tiki torches. Everything was already lit, casting the patio in a soft glow.

We settled into teak chairs with a small table between us.

"Gia Santella. When they told me about you, they forgot so many important details."

I didn't answer.

"Your beauty, yes. But what you have is more compelling than beauty. You have something else. I've met the most beautiful women in the world. But you have something they don't."

I was tempted to roll my eyes. Dude could lay down the lines like a master fisherman.

Instead of acknowledging his words, I reached for my wine glass and took another sip.

But this time he didn't speak first. I waited. Finally, I turned to make sure our eyes met as we spoke.

"It is true. I do have something else they don't have."

He exhaled audibly, instantly picking up on my meaning.

"Yes."

"She is happy with me."

"I can see why she would be," he said.

"I would die for her."

His eyes bored into mine as if he were searching the very depths of my soul. I did not look away. I wanted him to see that I meant what I said. I wanted him to feel my sincerity deep down inside his being. His eyes slightly widened, and he nodded very slowly.

"Yes. I believe that." He stood. "I think dinner is ready. We will eat at the kitchen table. The formal dining room is a bit dreary. I usually serve meals there with people I don't really care for."

He walked in without waiting for my answer, leaving his wine glass on the table. I picked up both our glasses and followed, perfectly aware that it meant I had no free hand to fight or defend myself. And still I didn't hesitate.

The weight of the gun in my bag as it slapped against my hip brought me comfort.

I put our wine glasses down on the table and turned to the kitchen island. Nico handed me a small, colorful ceramic bowl with some of the salsa and a larger matching bowl filled with tortilla chips. I brought them to the table, and he soon joined me, bringing with him the strips of steak and a warm stack of soft corn tortillas.

I hung my bag from the back of the chair as we sat down.

"Not bad," I said after I'd had a few bites.

He burst into laughter. "That's it? Not bad. I suppose you are naturally a gourmet chef, being Italian-American?"

"Nah," I said. "I can barely boil water. But my father was an amazing cook. And my friend...." I stopped. I'd almost said Dante's name.

"Oh, yes," he said with a knowing smile. "Dante is an excellent cook. His restaurants have all received the James Beard award."

My appetite was gone. I set down my fork and knife. My face felt icy cold.

"Yes, Gia. I know much about you and who you care for and how you spend your time. As I've told you—it's my job to know things."

"What are you intending to do with those things you know?"

"That depends on you," he said, and speared another slice of steak and tortilla onto his fork. He chewed it and watched me.

I took my bag off the back of my chair and set it in my lap. I watched his eyes as I unzipped it to see if he would stop me. He appeared uninterested in what I was doing, blotting his mouth with a cloth napkin. Inside my bag, my fingers brushed up against the cold handle of my Glock. I withdrew a battered silver cigarette case and took out my pack of Dunhill blues. He watched me as I placed one between my lips and then leaned over one of the small votive candles to light it.

I inhaled and scooted my chair back from the table, leaning back into it and watching him wordlessly.

He oozed power in a way I'd never experienced before. I'd met some of the most evil and powerful men in the world. One man I'd fallen hard for had been a Silicon Valley founder who was going to build the first apartment complex to orbit the moon. He'd had world leaders in his pockets. But this man. This man's power was something beyond even that.

It wasn't that he knew details about me and my life. Anyone could unearth those facts. It was the fact that under his tutelage, billions of dollars of drugs flowed throughout the Americas and beyond.

"How can you live with yourself?" I said, exhaling above the table and reaching for my wine glass. I kept my eyes trained on him as I sipped. I didn't need to elaborate.

"It's going to happen regardless of whether I'm involved—or even alive," he said.

"That's not an answer," I said.

He pushed a small ceramic dish toward me and looked at the long ash hanging from my cigarette.

I ashed my cigarette and waited. He reached over to my cigarette case and placed his hand on it, raising an eyebrow. I pushed it toward him.

He lit a cigarette and exhaled before answering.

"A boy born into the slums of Guatemala did not have many options to get to where I am today," he said, looking off into the distance as if he were remembering.

"And once you are there, are you trapped? Is it a prison?"

"One with golden bars," he said smoothly.

"Must be rough," I said.

"I live a very simple and frankly, lonely, life."

"Is that why you decided that you suddenly want Rosalie? You want a daughter to keep you company?"

Anger flared in his eyes, and he pushed his plate away forcibly.

"You are not stupid. You know that I was lied to. You know that I didn't even know Rosalie was alive."

"True," I said, lightly. "But do you want a kid because you are lonely? Do you think it will bring you permanent company? Someone who *has* to stay with you?"

I could tell he was trying to control himself. My words had pissed him off. Good. Now that I had my handbag in my lap, the weight of my Glock was reassuring.

"I am her father," his voice was louder than I'd ever heard it to that point. And powerful. I suddenly saw the cartel boss in all his glory.

"And you think that means something to her? Or to me?" I said.

He pounded his fist on the table and half-rose. "You are Italian. You know that *familia* is everything. You know. Don't play stupid with me." The angrier he got, the more his accent stood out. I hated myself for liking the way it sounded.

I took out my gun and set it on the table, pointing it at him. "I came here to tell you to leave her alone."

He didn't even look at my gun.

"If I disagree?"

"You die," I said.

"I don't believe you," he said. "You are not a killer like me. Do you know they call me that? *Asesino a piedra fría*?"

I shrugged.

"You will have to kill me to stop me from getting Rosalie. She is mine," he said.

"Okay."

He laughed. "You do not have the killer instinct."

"I've killed before. I took out three of your soldiers in California, remember?"

To his credit, he winced.

"Yes," he said. "But you would not kill an unarmed man who just made you the most delicious meal you've had in ages. I dare you. Shoot me. Now. If you do, you can have Rosalie."

"I had better last night," I said and squeezed the trigger. I aimed for his shoulder, near the collarbone. Red blossomed on the white shirt. The force pushed him back in his chair.

"*Mierda*." He grimaced but did not get up or even reach for his shoulder to staunch the bleeding. "Well?" he said. "Are you going to finish what you started?"

I hated to admit it, but his tone was triumphant.

"If I don't, will you kill me?" I asked. "Do I have to kill you to keep Rosalie?"

He shrugged. "If I didn't kill you, people would no longer fear me."

I set my gun back down on the table.

"You're right," I said, standing and turning toward the kitchen island. "I'm not a cold-blooded killer."

It was a gamble. But he had to take me seriously. He had to know I was not afraid of him. If I didn't convince him, he would never give up on Rosalie. He remained seated. He hadn't even reached for the gun.

"I'm not a cold-blooded killer," I repeated. "And neither are you."

"You are wrong," he said.

"The gun's right there," I said.

"How do you know I won't shoot you in the back?" he asked. "And what on earth are you doing anyway?"

I was opening drawers in the kitchen one after the other as fast as I could.

"Looking for something to stop that blood," I said.

"Under the sink," he said.

I found a small first-aid kit under the sink by a fire extinguisher. He was still sitting at the kitchen table, but he'd at least pressed his linen napkin to his shoulder to staunch the bleeding.

The gun remained on my side of the table where I'd left it. I walked over with the first-aid kit and pulled a chair up close to his side. I leaned down and unbuttoned his shirt, trying not to think about the fact that he smelled really good. Some spicy cologne mixed with pure male scent. After his shirt was unbuttoned, I drew it back, taking the napkin he was holding away. I took a quick look at the flowing blood before pressing a small, clean square of gauze onto the wound. It was immediately soaked through. I grabbed another wad of gauze and pushed with both palms on it, leaning my body into it to stem the flow.

He was losing too much blood.

"You feeling okay?"

He shrugged, then winced. "Would be a stupid way to die, bleeding out from a bullet to the shoulder in my own kitchen."

"You're going to need a doctor," I said.

"She's on the way." His cell phone rested on the table. I hadn't seen him do anything.

"What are you going to say to her?" I said.

"It was an accident."

"She'd better hurry," I said, replacing the gauze with another one that immediately soaked through.

"That was cute, though," he said, looking at the first aid kit. "How you thought you could patch me up all by yourself."

I made a face.

The doctor arrived less than a minute later with two male nurses. I used the code to let them in. She barely glanced at me and then rushed into the kitchen. She was older and rather large with a stethoscope around her neck. She was wearing a lavender velour tracksuit.

The two men carried Nico into a small bedroom off the kitchen. I heard him exclaim loudly in a litany of Spanish curse words. I paced in the kitchen. None of this, not one single fucking second, had gone as I'd planned. I had no idea what to do next.

Finally, the doctor came out. She handed me some pills.

"Make sure he takes these when he wakes. They will fight infection. I gave him something to help with the pain and make him sleep."

I wordlessly took the pill bottle and watched as the two nurses filed out after her, closing the door behind them.

I could hear *El Jefe's* snores erupting from the open door of the darkened bedroom.

What the fuck? I came to kill him or be killed, and now I was his goddamn nursemaid.

ONCE AGAIN, TIME TO PIVOT. BACK TO THE ORIGINAL PLAN.
All was good. He was nothing if not patient.
Patience and persistence had served him well thus far.
It was the secret to success.
That and faith in the outcome.
And he had nothing but faith.
Full confidence.

I waited for two hours and *El Jefe* was still out. I had already snooped—oops, *explored*— the entire house. Part of me was tempted to just leave him there alone. But we still had unfinished business.

I had immediately headed to the very masculine master bedroom on the top floor. It was within a small penthouse. The bedroom was taken up by a king bed with a dark brown leather headboard. I flipped on a light switch and hidden lights under the bed's raised platform turned on. I flopped on the bed. I was tempted to close my eyes but knew I would fall asleep within seconds.

Better to stick close.

In his walk-in closet, I found a pair of silver silk pajamas. I stripped and slid them on. The pants were too long even if I rolled the waist over several times. I tried to cuff the pant bottoms but the silk material wouldn't stay up, so I settled on wearing the pajama top alone, which was long enough to be a nightgown anyway.

Back downstairs, I went to check on Nico. Still asleep. His breathing seemed less frenetic, though. I was so damn tired. I brought the gun in from the kitchen and set it on the nightstand before I crawled into the bed with him and slipped under the covers. I lay on my back staring at the dark ceiling, wondering what on earth was going on. But nearly as soon as I thought that, blackness closed in on me.

————

I WOKE up startled and disoriented, sitting up and pushing bed covers off of me. I jumped when I felt someone at my side. I looked over to find *El Jefe* calmly watching me.

"*Buenos dias,*" he said.

I was already out of the bed. In the kitchen, I retrieved a glass of water and the pill bottle. Back in the room, I shook out two pills and handed them to him with the glass held out. He put the pills in his mouth. I watched as he struggled to sit, reaching for the glass of water. He winced in pain and lay back, groaning.

"Here." I cupped my hand behind his head and lifted it up to meet the glass of water in my other hand. He took a quick sip and leaned back.

"Thanks."

"Yeah."

"I've never loved my pajamas more," he said, glancing at me. The shirt had pushed back as I sat on the edge of the bed revealing most of my thigh. I quickly stood.

"Will you sign something that gives me custody of Rosalie and in which you agree to never try to come after her?"

He frowned. "No. Of course not."

"She's mine," I said.

He exhaled loudly. "Gia, you have to give her to me. Or I have to kill you."

I reached over to the nightstand and handed him the gun.

He shook his head. He knew as well as I did that he wasn't going to kill me. I didn't know why, but I knew this.

"There is no way to resolve this," he said. "We are both very stubborn people, aren't we?"

I chose my words carefully. "Now that I've met you, I see you're not a monster."

He raised an eyebrow but did not speak.

"I think you probably do want Rosalie in your life for all the right reasons," I said and paused. "But here's the thing. She has a good life with me. She has a normal life. She goes to school. She has friends. She has a dog. She is learning to play the saxophone. She is happy. And safe."

"The saxophone, heh?" He bit his lip.

"You cannot provide her with those things."

"I am her father," he said in that same booming voice from the night before. "I am her blood."

"But she will be in danger if she is with you," I said. "She is safe with me."

"That is not true."

"The price on your head, the life you lead—you are living by the sword, and you will die by the sword. This little girl deserves better."

What I said must have struck home because I saw him swallow hard and look away.

Triumph filled me. I had appealed to his humanity. His caring as a father. With words that were true: Rosalie deserved to be kept safe and deserved better than life with one of the world's most notorious criminals.

He cleared his throat and met my eyes. "Are you safe here with me?"

I looked around. Nobody was getting into that house without him knowing. He had an army, hell a SWAT team, at his disposal.

"I asked you," he said. "Do you feel safe?'"

I nodded.

"If I make you feel safe when I really don't care if you live or die, do you not think I would do everything in my power to keep my own daughter—my own flesh and blood—safe?"

For whatever stupid reason, him saying he didn't care if I lived or died stung, but I ignored it and said, "What kind of life is that? Would she be a prisoner? Would she be able to go to school like a normal girl? Would she have to memorize a code to go outside and play every day?"

It was slightly hypocritical because my own loft had top-notch security, but I didn't care.

He reached for my hand. I started to draw back in surprise, but then let him take it in his. He began to caress it. That's when I yanked it back.

Suddenly I realized that the dangerous current of tension between us since we'd met held a massive element of sexual attraction. Oh fuck.

"She has you. And she is very lucky," he said. "But she also needs a father."

I stood. "I need coffee. Stat. Otherwise, I'm going to get crabby as fuck, and you won't like anything I have to say."

He laughed.

In the kitchen, I found coffee beans, a grinder, and a French press. I returned to the bedroom to find the bed empty. A small door was open, and I saw *El Jefe* in the doorway of a small bath-room. He was buck naked. I realized he'd been naked in bed beside me all night long. *Well. Well.*

He walked back to the bed, not the slightest bit self-conscious, and I watched him sit and pull on loose pajama pants that rested on a nearby chair. He looked at a T-shirt on the chair.

"I don't think I can put that on."

"I don't think so either." I ran up to the master bedroom and came back down with a black button down shirt. I helped him slip it on and button it up.

"Doctor Yvonne said the bullet went in and out. Under the clavicle and out to the side of the scapula. Missed an artery by this much," he held out his fingers a half-inch apart. "I should be back up to speed in the next day or two."

"Huh," I said. "I thought I was a better shot than that."

"Apparently not," he said.

———

HE LOOKED at the tray I'd prepared. "If you wouldn't mind carrying that up to the upper deck, I'd love to take my morning coffee with you up there. Most mornings the dolphins come to visit and put on quite a show."

Settled into the patio on the upper deck, we sat side by side facing the sea, sipping coffee and breaking off pieces of some *pan dolce* I'd found in a paper bag on the counter.

"There!" he said, exclaiming and pointing with his uninjured left arm. He handed me a small pair of binoculars.

Sure enough, there was a small pod of dolphins playing in the surf, leaping up in what seemed like sheer joy. They seemed smaller than I would've thought they'd be, but the binoculars helped me see them even better.

"Wow," I said. "You see them every day?"

"About every other, but that's amazing in itself, no?"

"It's pretty cool," I said.

We sat in companionable silence. I hated how easy it was to be around him.

At one point, our thighs brushed against one another as I leaned over to put the binoculars down. Everything about sitting there felt good—drinking strong coffee, eating sugary bread, and feeling the warm sun on my bones as I looked out at the water. I felt safe.

When his left hand landed on my thigh, I didn't move it away. I didn't move when his hand found its way high up under the silk pajama shirt. Soon I was straddling him on the wooden chair. I then proceeded to make sure he forgot about any pain I'd caused him the night before when I put a bullet in him.

36

WHILE NICO TOOK A SHOWER, I SAT IN HIS BACKYARD ON A LOUNGE chair smoking and trying to figure out what the fuck had happened over the past twenty hours. I was in this beach village to do one of two things: talk *El Jefe* into giving up his quest to take Rosalie from me or—if that didn't work—kill him.

So far, neither were even a remote possibility.

I'd had the chance to kill him. But I had to admit that I didn't want to. My entire being rebelled against that option. I knew if I absolutely had to, I *probably* could do it.

The thing was, he hadn't made it necessary.

He wasn't going to kill me, so I didn't need to kill him first.

And what, I was going to walk into his beach house and shoot him dead between the eyes because he wanted his flesh-and-blood daughter in his life?

Fuck. Fuck. Fuck.

This was a major clusterfuck without any clear answers.

I looked at my bag on the tiny wrought iron table beside me. My gun was still inside. I wished I had my phone. I needed advice. But what was Dante going to say? He'd say I was fucking losing it.

And Eva, my aunt? She was a trained assassin. She'd wonder why the hell *El Jefe* was still alive.

No, I was on my own.

I had to figure out how to proceed. I needed a plan.

But I had nothing. Zip. Zilch.

And, worst of all, I really wanted to go back inside and fuck him again. Even thinking it made me squirm in my seat. I loved sex. And I used to have a lot of it before Rosalie was in my life. And goddamn it, I missed it. And that was okay. It was natural and beautiful and really, really, really good with the man inside the house.

He was obviously not a monster.

But even though I was extremely attracted to him, it didn't mean anything when it came to Rosalie.

Her well being was more important than my own life.

I was all she had.

I stubbed out my cigarette.

That was it. I knew what to say and do.

37

WE WERE WALKING DOWN THE BEACH ON THE WET SAND, WHICH made the going a little easier.

Only once did he wince when I brushed his side by accident.

"You cool?" I asked. It'd been my idea to take a walk. He'd readily agreed. "You're not in pain, right?"

"I'm good," he said. But I couldn't see his eyes behind the dark sunglasses. They had been the only thing he'd grabbed, along with a key to the back gate leading to the beach.

I'd slung my purse over my shoulder.

We'd nearly reached the end of the beach that met the rocky point. It was nearly time to turn around.

"You take me down here to whack me?" he said.

"Whack you?"

"Yeah, isn't that the term they use in the Godfather? Or maybe the Sopranos?" He had a mischievous grin on his face.

I rolled my own eyes, even though I knew he couldn't see them through my dark sunglasses.

He laughed. But then grew serious.

"You know why didn't you kill me when you had the chance?" he asked again.

"I know, I know. Because I'm not a killer like you," I said in a sing-song voice. "But the real question is, why haven't you killed me?"

I stopped and turned. He pulled up to a stop as well. He turned to face me, razing his hand through his thick head of hair while seemingly staring out at the ocean.

"Because I'm a foolish old man who's lost the touch," he said.

"How old are you?" I suddenly wanted to know. Partly because I wondered if he was the oldest man I'd had sex with, but also because I wanted to know how much longer he would live. What if he was, like, in his 70s and could die any day? What would happen to Rosalie then if he somehow got her from me?"

"I'm 53."

I didn't answer. Definitely the oldest man I'd ever had sex with.

"Old, right?" he said.

"Does your family have a history of dying young? I mean do you have like cancer or other diseases that run in your family that increase your chances of dying in the next few years?"

"You *do* care," he said.

I scoffed. "I'm thinking of Rosalie. What if she grows attached to you and then you up and die on her."

"What?" He frowned. "What are you trying to say?"

"Here's the way I see our situation," I said. "You want Rosalie. I want Rosalie. But what does Rosalie want?"

I paused. He started working his lip with his teeth as if he were thinking.

"If she went to live with you, what kind of life would she have? And what if you die in the next few years, then what does she have?" I said.

He swallowed. "I've thought of these things."

"And?"

He shrugged. "I don't know."

"Can we both agree that we want what is best for Rosalie? That is not in dispute?"

"Agreed," he said. "But I also have to find out if what's best for Rosalie might be having her father in her life. I can't assume that her current situation is what's best for her. I need to know if my involvement in her life will be a positive or a negative. I can't die not knowing that."

"You're dying?"

"No. I mean no, not right away—unless the doctor told you something you're not telling me."

We both laughed.

This time I turned toward the sea and looked out at the vast horizon. I spoke without turning toward him. "I have an idea."

"Go on."

The sound of a boat came to me at the same time. *El Jefe* yanked me by the arm and ran, dragging me with him toward the rocky outcropping on the point.

"What the fuck?" I complained but ran with him.

He pulled me down behind a large rock just as a spray of bullets struck the rocks behind and above us, sending sharp splinters of granite raining down on us.

"Give me your gun," he said.

I handed it to him, and he poked his head above the rocks only to quickly duck back down as gunfire erupted again.

He pulled a phone out of a pocket. I heard voices in the distance, and the sound of the boat's engine stopped. *Oh shit.* They were coming to shore.

El Jefe dialed a number and spoke rapidly in Spanish. I could make out a few words and phrases, such as "at the point" and "guns" and "cartel."

He hung up and tucked the phone back in his pocket.

"Just so you know?" I said. "This isn't convincing me that Rosalie would be safe with you."

He shook his head. "This is a minor problem. It's the Rivas Cartel thinking they can get the avocados away from me."

Avocados? "You're fucking kidding, right?"

"No," he looked surprised at my reaction.

"You mean opioids, hashish, cocaine, right? Not avocados. Or is avocados a euphemism for something else?"

He smiled. "No. Avocados."

I stared at him, speechless. He poked his head back up over the rock and dipped it back down. "They are on shore now. One is busy with the boat. We should make a run for it." He gestured behind us to a larger outcropping of boulders.

Unfortunately, we were at the worst possible spot to be confronted. The end of the beach was in a sort of sheltered pocket. The road that ran parallel to the beach through most of the village was now about twenty feet above us, up a craggy, inhospitable hillside. And the sand basically dead-ended at the rocky outcropping, which was also impossible to scale.

There was a small opening between two rocks in our little hideaway, and by crouching down I could see out to the water. Two men were standing in front of a motorboat that had been pulled up onto the shore. They stood with guns pointing toward us. I ducked back behind the larger rock.

Two. We were evenly matched. For what it was worth.

Nico stuck his head up above the rock again and quickly drew it back.

Another volley of gunfire rang out, striking the rock in front of us and above.

"Did you call for someone to come help us?"

"They are too far away."

I thought about that for a second.

"What's the plan, *El Jefe*?" I said. He shot me a glance of annoyance. I knew it was because of the name.

"On my count of three, we stand, you turn and run toward the rocks. I will cover you," he said.

I looked behind me. The last thing I wanted to do was turn my back on two gunmen and run, but I didn't think I had much choice. We had to put some distance between the men and us, and the rocks behind us would give us much more shelter and room to maneuver.

"One."

I got to my feet and crouched.

"Two." I put my hands on my knees in a sprinter's pose. As I did, I saw him reach down underneath his pant leg and withdraw another small gun. *What the fuck?*

"Three," he said and I bolted, sprinting at a crouch toward the outcropping of rocks behind us and zigzagging a bit. I heard a volley of gunfire behind me and half expected to feel bullets piercing my back any second, but I made it behind the rocks a few seconds before Nico ducked in beside me. We were both breathing heavily.

I straightened and found that in our new location I could fully stand without exposing myself. I knew that sometimes people who'd been shot didn't even realize it at first, but after a quick check of my body, I relaxed. I looked at Nico. He was crouched slightly with his hands on his knees catching his breath. When our eyes met, we both smiled.

"Did you hit them?"

He shook his head. "No. But I got us here."

"True." I peeked out. "Now what?"

"My men should be here soon."

"I thought you said they weren't close."

"Well, they were ten minutes out."

"What? Are they usually much closer?"

He nodded. "Yes. I always have bodyguards. Always."

"Except last night and this morning?"

He looked away. "Yes. Except for last night and this morning."

"In honor of my visit?"

"I thought it would be more conducive to an honest conversation if I didn't have my men eyeballing you."

"Eyeballing?"

"They would be suspicious of any move you made."

"Aha."

"Would they have watched us fuck?" I said.

"Fuck?" He said the word with a frown as if it were distasteful.

I didn't answer. That's what it was. What did he think I should call it? Making love? Hardly.

He didn't answer. Instead, he busied himself by slowly poking his head around the side of a rock. Shots rang out, and he drew back quickly. I stared, waiting for him to answer. When he didn't, I finally caved. "Would they have? Watched us?"

"Yes."

"Fuck," I said and saw him wince. He obviously wasn't used to a woman who swore like a truck driver. But his answer had me thinking. "Did they watch you with—"

"No," he cut me off. "When I am with someone I trust, they do not watch."

"You do not trust me?"

He laughed. "Why should I trust you? You shot me in the shoulder."

"Grazed," I said. "Let me get this straight—you always have bodyguards in your house at all times. Always?"

"It's how I avoid getting myself into situations like this one," he said.

"Fair enough," I said.

The phone rang. He picked it up and listened and then said, "Yes. Very well."

He hung up and said, "They are coming by air."

"You're kidding?"

"No."

As soon as he said it, I heard the whirring vibration of a helicopter approaching.

"Look," *El Jefe* said and stepped out from the cover of the rock.

I followed him warily, keeping most of my body shielded at first until I saw what he was talking about. The two men were kicking up sand and racing back toward the boat.

"Do they think a helicopter can't follow a boat?" I said. But then I noticed that the helm of the boat held a small machine gun. That had been the first sound of shooting I'd heard when the boat had approached the shore.

The bone-thudding chop of the helicopter was right on top of us, but I couldn't see anything. Then it rose like a specter above the rocky outcropping beside us.

The two men reached the boat. One man hoisted himself into the boat and hopped behind the machine gun as the other pushed the boat with a thrust into the waves.

But by then the helicopter was upon them.

A man with a shotgun was leaning out the open door of the helicopter. He picked the men off one-by-one. They crumpled into the boat where I could no longer see them.

The phone rang again.

Nico's face scrunched as he tried to listen over the noise of the helicopter, which was now leaving, heading back over the rocks from where it had come.

"Yes. Give us five minutes." He hung up and reached for my hand with his right one. I noticed a splotch of blood was seeping through his shirt's fabric at the shoulder. That's when I realized he'd fired the two guns using both hands.

He tugged at me and started walking back along the beach

in the direction of his house. About five minutes later, we reached a spot where the beach was once again at the same level as the road that ran parallel to it.

A big dark SUV pulled up, and we hopped in the back.

He strapped on his seat belt. I didn't.

I turned my entire body to him.

"Let's talk avocados," I said.

38

"IT IS A BILLION-DOLLAR INDUSTRY IN MICHOACÁN," HE SAID.

Michoacán was between this beach town and Mexico City, which was some 400 miles inland.

"You said *billion*. With a '*b*'?"

He nodded. "I'm sure you've heard stories of the violence in that area. It all stems from the war over the avocado industry. We'd taken it over last year. I didn't like how the Rivas Cartel was treating the workers. And the money was being funneled toward more drugs. So, we took over control of the industry. We keep it separate from the drug trade."

"And reaping some of those billions was no motivation at all for you, was it?" I said.

He ignored my sarcasm. "Recently, the Rivas Cartel has been intercepting our deliveries and killing our soldiers in very public and horrific ways. Not only to shame me, but to make me look bad to the rest of the world."

"Like what?"

"You heard about the dance floor?"

I squinted, remembering. When I did, my eyes popped open.

"The one where they rolled five heads onto the dance floor at that club?"

I didn't tell him that ever since Rosalie had come into my life, I had been paying a lot of attention to the news out of Mexico.

"Yes," he said and winced. "They were the heads of five of my top soldiers in Michoacán. It was before we knew they had moved in. It was an ambush."

I remembered hearing that there had been retaliation for those slayings. Five bodies had been strung up on a wall in town with a warning sign that *El Jefe*'s vengeance was swift and deadly.

It was tit for tat.

It was also, if I remembered correctly, what had prompted the president of Mexico to officially declare a war on drugs.

"That's your war?" I said looking at the driver's head in the front seat. If he was interested in what we had to say he was hiding it well.

"*Si*," he said. He'd slipped into Spanish.

"You are at war, and yet you want me to hand over a small child into your care?"

He sighed loudly, clearly exasperated.

"Yes, Gia. As I mentioned earlier, I am never without armed guards. My house in Mexico City is a fortress. Nobody can get within three miles of it without receiving a welcoming committee that would make your U.S. Special Forces team proud.

"I believe that," I said. "That's why I, um, decided to meet up with you here instead."

"She will be utterly safe. I pledge my own life to this."

"What kind of life would that be for her?" I said. "Locked in some mansion in Mexico City?"

He didn't answer. He just looked out the window.

We pulled up to the gates to his house. They opened and the SUV slipped into a subterranean garage.

Before he opened the door, he turned to me. "Would you care to visit my home in Mexico City?"

"Sure," I said. *Why not?*

The truth was, I had no idea what the hell I was doing in Mexico with Nico Ortiz Morales. I sure as hell wasn't talking him out of going after Rosalie. At least it didn't feel like it. Although he had paused when I asked him what kind of life he would be giving her as a prisoner in a Mexico City fortress. I'd keep pressing that point.

Since I was fairly confident I was not going to kill him unless he tried to kill me first, persuading him to see my side was my only hope.

39

ANTHONY WAS LIVID.

Nico didn't blame him.

The attorney called while Nico was in the car driving to his estate in San Miguel de Allende with Gia.

"I find it completely and utterly irresponsible and foolish for you to have dismissed your guards at the beach house. Do you have a death wish, Nico?" he said. He didn't wait for a reply, he just kept ranting. "You will not be a very good father to the child if you are dead. We spend hundreds of thousands of dollars each year to keep you safe. The budget for the security team we employ is insane. Not to mention, I spent the entire last week trying to make peace with the Mexican president who is ready to disavow you to curry world favor. And this is how you repay me? You thank me by nearly getting yourself murdered?"

Nico waited until Anthony had stopped talking, and the only sound through the phone was heavy breathing.

"It all turned out well," he said.

"That is all you have to say?"

"No. Any luck with finding some accountants for us to interview?"

Anthony exhaled loudly before answering. "Yes. I have three lined up. For next week. Thursday at ten. In your Mexico City loft. We will stay the night there Wednesday."

"Excellent," Nico said. "I will call the avocado attorney and tell her we will meet with her and her staff in two weeks' time."

"Maybe we should wait until the meeting with the accountants."

"No," Nico said quickly. "I'm done waiting."

"Very well."

"I'm on my way to the estate. But I have a guest. A woman. I would prefer not to be disturbed for at least the next forty-eight hours. Then I will meet you at the loft before our meeting."

"You have a guest? It's that woman, isn't it? What are you doing, Nico?"

"I know what I'm doing," Nico growled and shot an irritated glance at Gia.

"Just a second, Nico," Anthony said. Nico heard someone speaking to Anthony. The conversation was muffled. Then Anthony returned to the line. "I'm sorry but there is something pressing that cannot wait. I need you to come to Mexico City immediately. We can have the accountant candidates meet us tomorrow afternoon instead."

"What is it, Anthony? Why the urgency?" Nico was on alert, triggered by the tone of his attorney's voice.

"It has to do with Rosalie's mother and the family."

"Spill it," he said impatiently.

"I have someone here who claims you are not, in fact, Rosalie's father."

Nico's breath caught in his throat. His heart thudded in his chest. No. Impossible.

"What?"

"Please come immediately."

"I'll be there at four."

40

"THIS IS WHERE SHE WOULD LIVE," NICO SAID AS WE WALKED INTO his home.

The home wasn't actually in Mexico City, and it wasn't actually a house. It was a fucking luxury estate with breathtaking views.

We were in an area some 200 miles northwest of the capital city. This village was high above Mexico City, which I had just learned was nestled in an area called the Valley of The Damned.

During our drive, *El Jefe* explained that Mexico City lay in a highlands plateau that stretched across Mexico and was surrounded by mountains and volcanoes. The valley was the hub for ancient civilizations such as the Teotihuacans, Toltecs, and the Aztecs.

"I have a penthouse in the city, but I never stay there," he said. "It was mainly where Sylvia stayed when she went into the city. That is where I need to meet Anthony today. But first I wanted to get you settled in."

It was the first time he'd said his wife's name. I watched him out of the corner of my eye to see if he would seem weird when speaking her name to me. He didn't react at all.

This home in San Miguel de Allende was gorgeous. The property was gated and thick with trees. After we left the main road and entered a gate heavily guarded by at least four men, we drove another half mile to the top of a small hill where the house was, behind yet another gate and fence. More armed men were at this gate, and I could see several others stationed along the fence line to both sides.

"You probably need a nice piece of the avocado action just to pay for your small army of guards," I said.

To my surprise, he laughed and shook his head. "True. Very true."

There was a small space in front of the house where a car could park, but we dipped to the right and drove around the massive structure to an attached garage tucked at the back of the home. I craned my head to look up at the house above us. It was hard to tell, but it seemed like the top of the garage space might be a massive patio covered with potted palms and overlooking the valley below.

As soon as we walked inside, a man had taken Nico's arm and whispered in his ear.

"Excuse me just a moment, Gia. I have an important call I must take."

I wandered the first floor, admiring the art on the walls and the sculptures scattered strategically around on flat surfaces. I didn't know a ton about art, but it all looked fucking expensive. And tasteful.

Nico returned, looking as if he were now miles away. But still he smiled at me.

"My apologies. My attorney is very bossy. He demands I come immediately."

"You don't need to show me around," I said.

"Please. I am not a heathen," he said.

We stepped into an elevator with one of the armed guards

who stood with his arms crossed, face expressionless. He wore his rig on the outside of his shirt in case anyone had any doubt he was packing.

Nico ignored him entirely. I decided to follow suit.

The elevator doors opened up to a massive living room filled with plush seating arrangements, two fireplaces, and windows that offered sweeping views of the city below on one side. The arches between rooms were whimsical curves, and heavy wooden beams gave the room a slight cave like feel.

Nico turned to the armed man, who'd stepped out of the elevator with us.

"Please wait for us here as I give my guest a quick tour of this floor," he said.

The man nodded and leaned against the wall by the elevator door.

El Jefe gestured to the windows. "The glass is bulletproof," he said.

He led me through an ornate living room and into a kitchen that opened up into a massive interior courtyard filled with plants and fountains and mosaics inlaid in tables, walls, and the patio floor.

We walked to the center of the courtyard. Looking up, I saw that the second and third floors were rimmed by an open hallway looking down on the courtyard, but on the side facing the valley there was a solid wall.

"That is where the master suite and guest room are," he said, noticing my gaze. "They are separated from the rest of the estate for privacy and security. It also contains a safe room. Come, let's go into the kitchen pantry."

He led me through double doors to a large pantry and over to a tall metal rack of pots and pans along one wall. He pushed a small lever at the back of the rack and it swung forward revealing a door. "This is a secret staircase that leads to the safe room on the upper level or to the garage on the lower."

"You know people would kill for this information," I said.

He shrugged.

"Now that Sylvia is gone, you and my attorney and architect are the only ones who know about it," he said. "It would be easy to narrow down who the snitch was."

"True. That architect is sort of slimy," I said. He didn't respond.

"Speaking of my attorney, he wants to meet you," he said.

I was surprised.

"Anthony is, well, let's say, a bit abrasive at times, and he's not very happy that you are here with me."

"Thanks for the heads up," I said.

I followed him back through the living room to the elevator.

"You don't take stairs?"

He shrugged and stepped inside. I followed. The armed guard got in last.

This time he hit the button that said "P," which I assumed stood for penthouse.

"The floor between the main living area and the penthouse is for people like Juan here and others who are employed at the estate," he said. "My room is on the penthouse level. There are also two guest rooms. That is where you shall stay."

He led me straight from the elevator into a master suite—a large room with red velvet curtains on all four walls. One wall of curtains was intersected by French doors leading to a balcony. On the large balcony was a table and chairs to seat six, a fire pit, a few lounge chairs, and a view of the pool area below. The pool was a brilliant rectangle of turquoise. Beyond it lay a large pool house, and on the other side was an uninterrupted view of the valley below.

I saw movement down below and gasped. A sleek black

panther emerged from the jungle-like area beside the guest quarters and walked leisurely over to the pool where it dipped its head and lapped water.

"Why I don't chlorinate the pool this time of year," he said.

"What in the fuck is that?"

"She's magnificent, isn't she?"

"Is that why you didn't take me to the pool area downstairs?"

"Yes. I let her roam the grounds during the summer months. In the winter, she will often hibernate and stay in her cave, but during the summer, I like to have her near."

"That's the biggest water bowl I've ever seen for a pet," I said, then turned to him. "*Is* she a pet?"

He whistled and the beast's head snapped up to look at us.

"She is."

"Huh." I was rarely speechless.

"Of course, I would never let her roam once Rosalie moves here. She is fine in the jungle surrounding the estate. I've been lenient since Sylvia's passing. She was mainly Sylvia's pet, and she is lonely."

"I don't know what to think of any of this," I said, gripping the rail and staring at the beautiful wild animal below that was still looking up at us as her tail swished back and forth.

"I know I should put her in the zoo, but I just can't believe that life would be better for her," he said. "I have a good friend who is the director of the Mexico City Zoo. I suppose I should ask her."

Something in his voice when he said "good friend" let me know it was a woman even before he said "her."

He turned and went back into the house. I followed him. He walked out of the master bedroom and turned right. The door to the bedroom next to his was wide open.

"This is Rosalie's room."

The room was painted a light pink and contained a bed with

pastel bedcovers and a canopy. The bed was piled with stuffed animals. There was a matching vanity with a pink satin-tufted seat and a big oval mirror strung with Hollywood starlet lights. A small, delicate music box with a ballerina in a pink tutu sat on a dresser along with a silver hairbrush, comb, and matching hand mirror. Posters of unicorns and other magical creatures hung on the walls.

I looked at him in surprise.

He pressed his lips together and exhaled audibly before speaking. "As soon as I knew Rosalie was alive, I began making arrangements to bring her home. This had been my wife's office."

I waited a beat and then said, "Do you always get what you want?"

"Yes. Until I met you."

41

AFTER SHOWING ME MY ROOM, *EL JEFE* LED ME INTO A MASCULINE office on the main floor. It was all dark wood and worn leather. He gestured for me to sit on one of the two armchairs facing the desk. He sat beside me.

"This is where I do business."

"We're in here to do business?" I asked. "As opposed to the bedroom, which is for fucking?"

He winced again at the word.

I wasn't sure why I took such perverse pleasure in watching him squirm when I said "fuck." But I did. I'd found myself saying it instead of "making love" just to see his reaction. I didn't usually talk like that. Sure, I thought it, but usually restrained myself from saying it out loud by thinking of my Grace Kelly-elegant mother.

His cell phone dinged. He glanced down and then quickly typed something.

"Sorry about that," he said when he looked back up.

I shrugged and waited for him to speak. This was his play.

"I'd like to make you a business proposition," he said.

"I want, more than anything in the world, to be part of Rosalie's life," he said. "The only thing I want more than that is to ensure she has a *good* life."

I swallowed. Something about the sincerity of his words had gotten to me.

"I've done a lot of thinking since you came into my life," he paused.

Again, the way he phrased it sparked something inside me: "came into my life" implied something positive, didn't it? Or was that wishful thinking on my part. I was horrified at the thought. I suddenly cared what this murderer thought of me? And holy fucking shit—did I *want* him to like me? I was a disaster. Full stop.

"You know we agree on this," I said.

"After much thinking, I think the following things. One," he said, holding up a finger. "Rosalie is most likely very happy living with you."

I caught my breath, but he kept talking.

"She also has the right to get to know her father." He ticked the second point off on another finger. "Three, staying in your home, going to school, and maintaining her regular routine is probably what's best for her stability after such a rough young life."

Now, I was nodding enthusiastically. But he was not done.

"And, lastly, so let's make that four, she needs to also live with me some of the time so we can establish a relationship as father and child."

It sounded so clinical. But sort of made sense.

After getting to know Nico Morales, I no longer considered him a monster. And I genuinely believed him when he said the most important thing in the world to him was Rosalie and ensuring she had a good life.

He was proposing some sort of custody arrangement. The thought of having her away from me for extended periods of time felt wrong. It made my stomach clench in anxiety.

"Keep going," I said.

"What if," he said, shifting uncomfortably and not meeting my eyes. "What if—just entertain this thought for a second—what if you had her living with you during the school year and then during the summer she could come stay with me? Either here, or at the beach house or both or maybe even someplace safer. I could buy a house that would just be for the summer with her and have it be the most secure, heavily guarded home that ever existed."

He spoke rapidly, caught up in the idea, so when he stopped suddenly and stared at me, I was taken off-guard.

"Uh," I started, then closed my eyes. "Give me a second."

I opened my eyes and paced the office, afraid to speak, sick with anxiety over agreeing to let Rosalie live with this man for three months of the year. Even if he *was* her father.

Finally, I turned to him. "I don't know."

"Think on it overnight," he said, standing suddenly. "I have to leave for Mexico City. I will stay there tonight. I was going to ask you to come with me to show you the city, but I have a better idea if you are game."

"Lay it on me."

"My oldest and dearest friend from Guatemala, Ian, has messaged me that he is in town for the next few days. He has asked about dinner tonight. Here is what I propose. This man knows me better than my own mother. And yet, he is unfailingly honest, sometimes to his detriment. I propose you spend the evening speaking to him and having dinner in town here. San Miguel de Allende is known as one of the most wonderful cities in the world. I will tell him to answer all your questions in deadly earnest. After speaking to him and sleeping on it overnight, we can speak again?"

He waited.

"Okay," I said. "Let's do it."

.

42

Nico had settled me into my room on the penthouse floor. It had been used, he said, for his mother when she was still alive. It was decorated in forest green velvet: sumptuous curtains that draped to the floor, a green velvet headboard, and a green velvet throw over the bed's white coverlet. One wall was painted black and another wall had two large black-and-white framed photographs side-by-side. One of Frida Kahlo. One of Diego Rivera.

I'd just taken a shower and was still wrapped in the towel when there was a knock on the door.

"Gia?"

I let the towel drop to the floor and said, "Come in."

He opened the door and froze. Water dripped down my shoulders from my wet hair.

He was holding a big stack of clothing over one arm. Without looking, he dumped all the clothing articles on the chair beside the door and was in front of me, picking me up so quickly I squealed as he brought me to the bed.

"I thought you had to leave?" I said.

"I'm going to be late," he said hoarsely, and then we stopped talking.

Later, I propped myself up on the cushions. "What time was your meeting in Mexico City?"

"An hour ago."

"Oops."

He stood and I snuck a glance at him. He was in remarkably good shape. He groaned as he leaned over to retrieve his clothes from the floor. "Gia, you are such a distraction. I haven't worked out or done yoga for three days." He turned and winked at me. "But it's been worth it."

He paused at the door. "I hope this doesn't seem odd, but I think you and Sylvia were the same size, and I found these in her closet. Feel free to go in and see if there is something you might like more, but I know the restaurant Ian is taking you to tonight is one where women do wear long dresses."

"Thank you," I said, pulling the covers up to my neck and watching him.

"Okay, then," he said. "Until tomorrow."

It was only when I heard the elevator ding and watched the doors whoosh closed that I got out of bed.

———

THE DRIVER WAS right on time. I was told a car would arrive at seven o'clock and take me to the restaurant where Nico's friend would be waiting. I'd tried on a few of the dresses that Nico had brought me, finally deciding on a dark green velvet one in honor of my bedroom and his mother's most excellent taste. I didn't have a single piece of jewelry, which I thought was best, considering the sumptuous nature of the dress. It was a halter style with an open back that dipped almost obscenely low. I slipped on some flat sandals that didn't show under the hem. I grabbed my bag with some lipstick and the reloaded gun tucked inside.

In the back of the car, I began to get a little nervous and wished I'd had a drink before leaving. I was sure *El Jefe* had booze somewhere. But it would be okay. I could do this sober. I really should have my wits about me to grill this friend about Nico if I was seriously considering sending Rosalie to live with him at some point in the future.

Ian was waiting for me on the sidewalk in front of the restaurant. As soon as the car came to a stop, he opened my door for me and held out his hand.

He was much older than Nico. He was thin and balding and wore wire-rimmed glasses. He wore a tight black T-shirt under a black fitted blazer, designer jeans, and sporty designer sneakers with a thick sole. I liked him right away.

"*Mucho gusto,*" I said, smiling at him as I stood. Nice to meet you.

"*Encantado,*" he said. Charmed.

The restaurant was lovely—dark and filled with candles and funky stained glass chandeliers that looked a bit Dr. Seuss-ish. The food was even better. Gourmet Mexican food meant shrimp enchiladas, mini tortillas with dollops of sweet potato and chorizo filling on top, guacamole that tasted like cilantro and mint and lime all at once, and salty chips that were just what the doctor ordered. I hadn't realized I was ravenous until the food arrived.

We exchanged niceties until I'd had some of the food and an entire margarita.

Feeling no pain, I leaned in, smiling. "Tell me why I should trust *El Jefe.*"

He smiled back. "The man is salt of the earth."

"He is responsible for possibly thousands of deaths around the globe."

"Most indirectly."

"That's a bullshit excuse."

He sighed. "He has killed. It is true. His business has been drugs. That is true."

"Has been?"

"He is trying to move away from that. He is exploring other avenues of income, such as crops like avocados."

"Oh my God, the fucking avocados again?" I said waving my hand wildly and thinking I probably shouldn't have the second margarita the waiter was putting before me right then.

Instead of shocking him, my words made him burst into laughter.

"Yes, the fucking avocados," he said. "My friend sees this as an honorable way out."

"Really?" I was skeptical.

"My dear Gia, unless you have lived in our shoes, unless you grew up in our small village, it is probably going to be impossible for you to understand why Nico does what he does or why he did what he did."

I thought about that before answering. "I believe you are right."

"Without experiencing firsthand the poverty and hopelessness and sheer desperation that we did, you cannot understand how a life as the head of the world's most powerful drug cartel would be an impossible dream that he has fulfilled," he said. "Even eating in this restaurant was not something we could have imagined in our wildest dreams."

I swallowed. I could not possibly understand.

"So, ask me what you will, and I will try my best to vouch for my friend's character, but just know this: I have and will always —until the day I die—trust my life, and that of my dearest child to this man. I would entrust anything to him."

I spent the next hour learning about Nico's past. It was not pretty. It involved him figuratively crawling on hands and knees out of one of the world's worst slums. Going for days without eating. Seeing violence firsthand every day of his life.

They grew up in a rural area known as the "poverty belt" of the country where malnutrition of Guatemalan children is among the worst in the world. Kids, on average, only attend three and a half years of school, he said.

"He has been secretly funneling millions of dollars there over the past two years to help with poverty and illiteracy. I'm his point man in Guatemala. I am the face of the foundation doing so. It is slow going, even with the money he is giving us. We need much more," he said. "One of the projects we are working on is buying some of the agricultural businesses there. Coffee, sugar, bananas, and cardamom. We hire locally and can then also pour some of the profits back into the community for education and hunger relief."

I sat back and thought about this. He was right. I didn't have a fucking clue. I could never stand in *El Jefe*'s shoes. I could not possibly understand. What I was hearing, though, was that this drug cartel, murderer, and thief was giving back to the community.

It was complex and confusing. Like so many things in life.

At the end of the night, when Ian walked me to the car, I leaned over and kissed his cheek. "Thank you for your time," I said. "He is lucky to have a friend like you."

"*Opuesto*. I am the lucky one."

"Good night," I said.

Before the car door closed, he leaned over and said, "His greatest wish in life is to be a father. Just remember that."

Then he closed the door, and the car pulled away. I turned to look behind us and saw him standing there watching us drive away.

The house seemed lonely even though there were armed

guards at the entrance and even stationed in a chair outside the elevator on the top floor. The guard nodded to me when I stepped out of the elevator and jumped seeing him sitting here. Creepy. Is that what it would be like if Rosalie ever came here?

I ducked into my bedroom and deadbolted the door before I changed into a silky nightgown I found splayed across the bed. It still had tags on it. *El Jefe* must have had it delivered while I was gone. It was a soft white that made my tanned skinned seem even more bronzed. I slipped beneath the covers, sunk into the luxurious bed, and dialed Dante.

"Ciao bella," he said. "I'm so glad to hear from you. I was getting a little worried."

"Hey," I said. "Is Rosalie right there with you?"

"She is coloring with Eva."

Coloring? My assassin former mafia boss aunt? *Unbelievable.*

"I need your advice," I said. I told him everything that had happened and all I had learned since meeting up with *El Jefe*, leaving out only that we had fucked.

"Wow," he said when I finished.

"No shit."

"What do you want me to say, Gia?"

"I want you to give me the straight talk you always do."

"Well, first, I can tell by the way you talk about him that you've had sex with him, so your thinking is not clear."

Anger flushed through me, but I bit my tongue and remained silent. When I didn't respond, he continued. "Even with that said, from what you've told me, and from a man's perspective, a man who wants nothing more than to be a father himself, I think you need to figure out a way to give the guy a chance."

"What?" *A man who wants nothing more than to be a father himself.*

"We need to figure out a way to give him a chance. I can help you figure something out."

"I mean the part about *you* wanting to be a dad. Dante? When did this happen?"

"Matt and I had talked about it," he said in a quiet, somber voice. "But it's been on my mind since then a lot. And now, after spending time with Rosalie, I have realized even more that I want to be a father. And I would be a damn good one."

"Oh, Dante, you would be an amazing father," I said and felt tears forming.

"I am going to start looking for a surrogate mother," he said.

"Good," I said and was filled with excitement. "I can't wait to be an auntie."

He was silent for a few seconds. Then he cleared his throat.

"Gia? Would...would you?"

"*What*?" I shot out of bed. "Holy fuck. You can't lay this on me right now, Dante. Holy fuck." I was pacing the room like a wild woman. "I've got a lot on my plate right now. I have the fate of a little girl in my hands. I'm staying in a goddamn estate in Mexico owned by one of the most powerful drug lords in the world, and you are asking me about giving birth to a baby? What the fuck, Dante?"

He burst into laughter, which instead of making me angrier, completely diffused my panic. I started laughing as well.

"So, you're telling me I've got a chance," he said, reciting one of the lines from one of our favorite Jim Carrey movies.

"No!" I shouted, but it wasn't in anger. "Back to me. And Rosalie. How can we give him a chance?"

"I think that, first off, he needs to meet her."

"For sure," I said.

"And then see what Rosalie thinks."

"Bingo," I said. "I've seen where Rosalie would stay. Now he needs to see where she lives and meet her on her turf."

"Wait," Dante said. "You're asking the leader of Mexico's most powerful drug cartel to come visit you in San Francisco?"

"Damn right," I said. "If he's serious about being in Rosalie's life, he'll make it happen."

"That's the plan, then," Dante said, enthusiastically embracing my plan. "He comes to us. She meets him. She decides if she wants to go visit him."

"Right!" I said. "And the first visit, I get to go, too, and be there to make sure it is smooth and she is comfortable. And if that first short visit goes well, then maybe we can extend it and so on."

"Yep. That's the plan."

"It's fucking insane." I'd be making dinner for a drug king-pin. Inviting him into my home. Crazy town.

"It's totally insane," Dante agreed.

"Which is why it might just work," I said.

"Yep."

"I knew you'd give me good advice, Dante," I said, filled with relief. "I just didn't know you'd ask me to carry your baby during the same conversation."

"We'll talk about that later."

"Yeah, much later. Like when hell freezes over later."

"Love you, Gia."

"I love you, Dante."

43

I woke later in the dark, heart pounding, sitting straight up, disoriented. After a few seconds, I realized where I was. I was wide awake and alone in a giant house. Well, alone except for a few creepy armed men whom I didn't trust as far as I could throw them.

I grabbed a soft throw off an armchair and, wrapping it around my shoulders, stepped out onto the small wrought iron balcony overlooking the pool and the valley beyond.

The shimmering water of the pool sparkled in the moon-light. As my eyes adjusted, I realized what was causing the water to undulate. The black panther stood at one end, dipping its head into the water. Then, as if sensing me, it raised its head and seemed to look directly up at me. A chill ran down my spine. For the first time I wondered, completely irrationally, how high the giant cat could leap. There was a balcony below me that stuck out further than mine and then one below that. A truly talented and intelligent animal could use the balconies as steps right up to my floor. I laughed at the thought. In the quiet of the night, the sound rang out, and the giant cat responded in irritation, roaring and taking off toward the jungle area behind it, tail swishing menacingly.

I fell back asleep easily but then woke suddenly in the dark to the feeling of a hand clamped over my mouth. A voice whispered in my ear urgently:

"Don't move. Don't make a sound. There are assassins after Nico and now they are here to kill you. Follow me."

The voice was familiar, and this calmed me enough to stop struggling.

"It is Ian. They have killed the guards. I'm going to remove my hand. Do you promise not to scream?"

I nodded. The hand left my mouth, and I gasped for air.

"What about the secret passage and room?"

"No. Anthony knows about it. That is the first place they will look. They are waiting on the floor below. I managed to barricade the door to this floor, but they are getting something to blow it apart.

Anthony? I thought he was El Jefe's friend? Blow it apart? They?

"We will escape off the balcony and jump down to the pool. Follow me."

He headed to the balcony, holding my hand and tugging me after him.

"But...but the fucking black panther is down there. Out there."

"It will not harm me."

"What about me?" I whispered frantically.

He didn't answer.

He tossed a small rope ladder over the side of the balcony. Throwing one leg over, he began to climb down. I scanned the area surrounding the pool and, not seeing the large cat, followed. We managed to reach the patio before I heard a sound from the bushes near the pool house.

"It's okay," he said. "Follow me."

He led me, again by the hand, around the far side of the infinity pool where it seemed to drop off over the cliff.

Instead, there was a small ledge on the other side where water that lapped over the side of the pool gathered and was funneled back into the pool's filtration system. He stepped down onto the ledge, which was about three feet below the edge of the pool, and tugged on my hand for me to do the same. Beyond the small ditch-like gulley was about a foot of concrete and then a sheer wall of nothingness that dropped down into the valley below.

I tried not to look but felt dizzy just knowing it was there.

A noise erupted from the house as someone inside noticed us, and we both ducked as a volley of gunfire erupted.

Ian pulled me down to a crouch in the narrow ditch of water. The water lapped at my chest, and I shivered uncontrollably.

At the same time, we heard a preternatural growl that echoed through the night. Instinctively, I poked my head up and saw a man facing us with a large gun. A crouched dark and shadowy figure was coming in fast.

As the man raised the gun to fire at my head, the large cat pounced. There was a deadly snarl and roar, and the man screamed in pain and terror.

He and the large cat plunged into the pool with a splash. The water immediately turned red with blood that spread in a circle from where they had submerged.

Ian grabbed my hand and we ran, splashing through the ditch to the other side near the pool house. Within seconds, Ian jumped on a four-wheel, all-terrain vehicle and gestured for me to hop on behind him. The engine roared to life and we tore off into the jungle along a dirt path. I had my hands clasped around his waist and my face pressed into the back of his shirt.

It was only when we'd put some distance between ourselves and the house that I was able to breathe normally.

"What about the cat?" I said.

He didn't answer, just shook his head.

"What the hell is going on?"

"We're meeting Nico in town. He will explain all."

Nico? *Here*?

44

NICO CLASPED GIA IN A HUGE HUG AS SOON AS SHE AND IAN slipped into the small house in the downtown area. Relief filled him. He was crazy thankful that she was unharmed.

"I've been betrayed," he said. "I'm so sorry you were brought into this. It was Anthony. He has been trying to kill me."

Halfway to Mexico City, Nico had received a phone call from the manager of the financial group that handled his investments.

The man had apologized profusely for calling Nico directly but had decided it was worth the risk of angering the drug lord to confirm the transfer since it was such a large amount.

Nico had authorized no transfer. But maybe this had something to do with Anthony's maneuverings of Sylvia's accounts, which were separate from Nico's investments.

"I'm glad you called," he said. "I've been busy. Remind me what transfer you are referring to?"

It ended up that someone had used Nico's passwords and other security measures to authorize the transfer of his largest investment account of $500 million dollars into an offshore account. The transfer would essentially clean him out.

"The reason I'm calling is because when you set up your account, you ordered a personal call be made to you on any transfers of more than $50 million and that they be verified with your secret code."

"Yes," Nico said. "Thank you. Please cancel the transfer."

"Forgive me, but can you provide me with the code first?"

"Of course," Nico said. He rattled off the numbers of code in three parts, interspersed with other words throughout several sentences. It was set up that way to prevent anyone who might be listening from paying any attention to the numbers he said. To the driver, it sounded like this: "The appointment was for ten. I understand. But there are still four items to take care of. I think they said it would be done by the fifth."

Then, using the same precautions, all of his security passwords were changed.

As soon as Nico hung up, he told the driver to turn around and head back to San Miguel de Allende immediately.

Anthony had betrayed him.

Any meeting in Mexico City would involve an assassination attempt.

He'd hole up at his estate and figure out what to do next.

However, as soon as he thought this, he realized his home was a target. Which meant Gia was in danger. He dialed Ian.

"I will go there immediately," his friend had said. "We will meet at my place. Don't worry. I will keep her safe."

Nico was, nonetheless, sick with worry until Ian and Gia walked into the rental apartment.

"Why do you think he wanted me dead as well?" Gia asked now.

"I think he wanted to kill you and Rosalie," he said. "Or at least make sure nobody knew she was mine. He knows she would inherit everything I own. Well, anything left that he hadn't already taken. He was named the beneficiary of my estate when Sylvia died. I'd recently ordered him to make arrangements to change my will and name Rosalie as the recipient of my trust."

Before he finished, Gia was dialing her cell phone.

"You okay?" she said and then, "Rosalie? Okay. Good. Keep the doors locked. Tell Eva we were just attacked by one of *El Jefe*'s closest confidants. He knew everything. Tell Eva it's probably time to head home."

Gia hung up. "It's all good."

"Thank God," he said. He realized he'd been holding his breath until she hung up.

"He stands to inherit everything from you?" Gia asked.

"Yes."

Gia's face did something odd. It was a look he'd never seen before. It was pity and concern. Her voice was soft as she said, "I think you better look at whether he killed Sylvia, too, Nico."

Horror shot through him. She was right.

He hugged her close. She was patting his back. It felt good.

For so long, for so many years, he had been the one who everyone else turned to for comfort. And yet, here in this woman's arms, he let himself go. He allowed himself to sink into her embrace, as she—so much smaller and younger than him—gave him strength through her touch.

She held him and smoothed back his hair, her lips brushed his brow in the briefest kiss.

After a few seconds, he pulled back.

"Now that I know Rosalie is safe and you are safe, it's time to go find Anthony."

45

IF NICO THOUGHT HE WAS GOING AFTER ANTHONY ALONE, HE WAS crazy.

"Let's do this," I said.

"Gia?"

"I'm going to need at least two guns. I like something smaller with heavy fire power. Preferably a Glock or Ruger."

Nico stared at me for a few seconds and then said, "Okay."

I hid my smug smile.

"There is a place I think he might be staying."

Ian spoke up. "I just heard from your house manager," he said. "None of Anthony's men survived."

"That means he has no idea how it all went down."

"We need to spread the word," Nico said. "I'm dead. Gia's dead."

"I'm on it," Ian said. "Be back soon."

After Ian walked out, Nico began to pace the small space.

"The way I see it," I said. "He has to play it one of two ways."

Nico stopped pacing and turned to me.

I continued. "He puts on a show, grieves you publicly, vows to find who did this, and so on."

"Or," Nico says, nodding and cracking his knuckles. "He bails now. He puts the second part of his murderous plan in place and disappears."

"But if he does, he forfeits the money you left him in the will, right?"

"Right," Nico said, brow furrowed.

"You know him. Which card is he going to play, Nico?"

Just then Ian came rushing into the house. "Anthony's apartment in the city was firebombed."

Nico didn't even blink. "Was there a body inside?"

"Yes."

"Can it be identified?"

"They said it was burned too badly," Ian said, visibly shaken.

Nico turned to me. "Want to know what card he played? He played the joker."

According to Nico, if anything happened to Anthony, all his money would be funneled to a trust he'd set up, ostensibly, to help starving children in Guatemala. Anthony had talked Nico into doing the same. Nico's will actually said that if Anthony was not around to inherit Nico's fortune, all the money would go to this trust.

Nico opened his phone and tapped his fingers for a few seconds before thrusting the device at me. "Look at the name of the trust."

It said: The Patrón Partners.

"His favorite tequila."

"It's him," I said. "The trust is still him."

Nico turned to Ian. "Can I borrow your car? We need to get to the airport asap."

"How about a helo?" Ian said.

"You're kidding?" I said. Where was he going to get a helicopter?

"Give me ten minutes."

THE HELICOPTER LANDED in a private area of the airport, not far from where Nico kept his small Lear jet. He'd received a text on the flight over and had handed his phone to me to read.

It said that Nico's pilot and plane had taken off from the airport ninety minutes earlier with a flight plan that purported to have them landing in Chiapas a half hour ago. But airport officials said no plane had landed. It had possibly gone down somewhere in the jungle.

Once the helicopter took off again and we were walking toward a squat building, Nico told me he'd chartered a private plane to take us to Belize. Anthony had once mentioned that he dreamed of retiring on a remote island near there.

Five hours later, we landed at a small airstrip in Belize. Nico stood as we landed, crossing the aisle to peer out the windows until he shouted triumphantly. "Yes!"

Nico's own private plane was on the ground.

Inside the airport, we asked for directions and immediately headed to the office of the airport director and manager.

The director was a bearded man with dark skin and brilliant white teeth that made his smile contagious. He took us into his office and shut the door before he said that Nico's private plane had come in without authorization a few hours before. Shortly after it landed, coming to a stop at the far end of the runway near the jungle, armed soldiers had met the pilot. He had surrendered. He'd claimed he had no passengers. He said when he had heard of *El Jefe*'s murder, he had become scared for his life and fled. He was seeking asylum in their country.

The bearded man who'd said he was in charge of all airport affairs looked at Nico. "Clearly reports of your death were exaggerated."

"Mark Twain," Nico said and smiled.

Then he took out a thick wad of cash and peeled off several bills. "Would you mind allowing those rumors to stay circulating in your country for at least another day."

"Dead man walking," he said with a smile, scooping up the bills from the table.

"Do you think your men know who I am?" Nico asked.

"I don't think so. In fact, I was merely making an educated guess. I don't think anyone really knows exactly what you look like."

"Fantastic," Nico said. "If you could arrange for a car and maybe an armed guard, my partner and I would like to take care of some business in your country. We hope to be done by tomorrow, if possible, and then back on our way home. If I were trying to lay low in Belize, where would I go?"

"Easy. There is a new development that caters to expats on the north end of the island. It is difficult to get to, so it remains somewhat isolated. If you take a boat, you can cut at least an hour off your trip. Most people do that. Some, however, drive, and it takes longer. The current roads aren't well maintained, and the new roads aren't yet developed."

"That sounds like a good place to start."

"And it might be worth knowing that, just in case the pilot was lying about not having any passengers, my men searched the jungle area next to that end of the runway. They found tire tracks and what looks like a recent puddle of transmission fluid."

"He had a car waiting."

"A four-by-four vehicle, it appears, from the huge tire tracks."

"Which makes me think there would not be a boat involved in the trip."

"Can you arrange for us to be on a boat in the next hour?" Nico took out the wad of cash and again peeled off several bills and slid them across the desk to the man's waiting palm.

"Of course," the director said. And then he turned. "Thank you for your donation to our literacy campaign last year. It was very generous."

Nico gave a polite nod to acknowledge it.

"You have friends everywhere," I said.

"And enemies."

———

OUR BOAT KEPT CLOSE to the shore, often staying under the canopy of trees that overhung the areas without a beach.

At one point, the boat operator abruptly killed the engine and pointed, grinning.

A large gray shape was swimming toward us just below the surface. About two feet away from the boat, a snout with two dark wide nostril holes poked out of the water for a second. The holes closed and the nose dipped back down.

Manatee.

Then the creature stuck its head up enough to look at us, so we could see its eyes before it dipped back down. It did this a few times and then swam away.

"Just checking us out, I guess," I said.

The boat operator started the engine again, and we took off. Every once in a while, he would point to the shore or to the trees, alerting us to crocodiles in the water or on shore and a few monkeys screeching in the trees above.

Before long, we pulled into a small cove. A tiny dock stretched out about twenty feet. The boat operator had killed the engine as soon as we rounded the corner of the cove. He was paddling us the rest of the way in.

The shore contained about a dozen squat, white-stone struc-tures. Some were still under construction. The finished ones had small patios facing the cove. All of them were surrounded by lush tropical plants. The jungle seemed to lie directly behind all the homes.

Nico handed the boat operator some cash. "Can you meet us back here in an hour?"

"Yes."

Nico paused and then said, "If we are not here, wait ten minutes, and then go back to the airport director and have him call the police."

The man nodded, tucking the money into his shirt pocket.

Even though we had spoken in low voices, two heads peeked out of the door of the house closest to the dock.

Then a third.

This time, a body followed the head.

A man dressed in khaki shorts and a white T-shirt.

Anthony.

He was out the door and around the side of the house before our feet hit the dirt at the end of the dock.

Nico pulled ahead of me in the chase. Soon we were behind the row of houses, racing through a backyard area with a pool and patio and on a dirt path carving through the jungle.

The greenish light made it hard to distinguish shapes. Everything blurred into the object next to it. Bushes crowded each side of the path, creating a seemingly impenetrable wall. If Anthony had tried to break through, he would've left the carnage of broken foliage behind, so we kept running straight ahead. After about five minutes, the path opened up to a clearing. Nico pulled up short at the entrance, head swiveling. The trees formed a canopy above the clearing so the light was still a greenish hue. It was possible the noises had been there the entire run through the jungle, but when we paused, the insect and animal sounds rang out in a cacophony of noise that undulated around us.

Nico's body heaved with exertion, but he was not panting

loud enough for me to hear. I was trying to catch my breath without making any noise, as well. My ears were alert to any possible sound indicating which way Anthony had run. Then Nico jutted toward one section of the clearing with his chin. I saw what he meant. A few bushes there had bent branches. He'd gone that way. As we raced across the open space and grew closer, I saw that from this angle there was a small path carved out right there. Nico plowed through it, and I was right at his heels, trying to stay closer this time. It was less than five minutes to the next clearing, this one much smaller. We were about to enter it when Nico stopped so suddenly I smashed into his shoulder. He crouched and held up a hand behind him. Instinctively, I crouched as well and then poked my head over his shoulder.

There was a large animal coming through the bushes somewhere close. My heart raced in fear.

Then I heard the click. It was the safety of a gun being released. It came from the side of us. I turned to see Anthony holding a gun, pointing it right at Nico's temple.

"If you hadn't come here, everything would've been just fine," he said. "You could have arisen from the dead and gone on to rebuild your empire, Nico. Why did you have to chase me down? Why couldn't you let me live in peace?"

Nico turned his head so the gun was aimed at his forehead.

"You don't deserve to live in peace."

"I have given my best years to you. Now it's my turn."

"Anthony, I would've given you anything you wanted," Nico said. His voice was a mixture of disappointment and grief. "I would have handed you $5 million to come live here like a prince instead of a fugitive like you are now. Why didn't you come to me?"

"I don't believe you."

"What have I ever done to cause you to doubt?" Nico said.

Anthony's face scrunched up. He looked uncertain. He didn't answer. I saw him swallow. The gun in his hand was shaking.

"Anthony?" Nico said. "Put the gun down. We can work this out."

"I didn't want to kill you," he said. "Or Sylvia." He let the name hang there and seemed to be searching Nico's face, which remained expressionless.

"Then why?" Nico asked.

"You have grown soft. You are weak. The last time I saw you act in a way befitting of your position was when you went to war with the Rivas Cartel to stop the sex trafficking in Cabo San Lucas."

"What are you trying to say, Anthony?"

"They wanted me to work for them. They have paid me good money. For your death."

"So you can live here?"

As he said it, I saw movement behind him. Something large, creeping up. I tapped my foot against Nico's in a warning. He gave me a side-eyed look and a tiny nod. He'd seen it too.

"This is one of my many homes, you fool," Anthony spat the words out. "I am staying here while they outfit my island. My own goddamn island, Nico. Can you say you ever had the same?"

It was a massive leopard. And it was ready to pounce.

"If they paid you enough to buy an island, why did you need my money too?"

"I need enough to live comfortably for the rest of my life."

He'd just said the word "life" when the big cat pounced on his back.

Anthony was suddenly flat on the ground and the cat was biting in a frenzy. Blood was flying everywhere. He'd gone right for the back of Anthony's head, taking a chunk out of it.

Anthony was not moving.

I was frozen with fear until the cat looked up with a bloody mouth and stared right at us. Anthony's body lay between us, but it wouldn't take much more than a hop for the cat to clear it.

Nico reached behind his back and grabbed me by the wrist. He hissed. "Whatever you do, don't run. It will trigger the panther to chase and attack."

I was shaking. "Okay."

"We are going to back off very slowly now. Stand as tall as you can. Raise your arms above your head like this." He let go of my wrist and raised his arms up like he was going to do a free throw on the basketball court. "I'm going to start yelling and being very loud," he was already speaking in a loud voice. We were already shuffling backward, putting more space between us and the large cat. And Anthony's body.

The big cat's tail was swishing, and it looked pissed off.

"Keep walking back," Nico said. "You don't even know what kind of crazy I am!"

Now Nico was shouting. If it weren't so terrifying—if Anthony's brains weren't spilling out of the back of his head—it would've been comical.

"Back off!" he shouted. "Go eat your dinner and leave us alone. We mean you no harm."

I was trying really hard not to judge what was coming out of Nico's mouth. Who the hell knew what I would say if I were him. Probably something with the word fuck in it a few times. But it was working. At least the cat wasn't coming toward us. It dipped its head to Anthony, its meal, and then looked back up.

Soon we could only barely see its eyes. That's when it seemed to forget about us. It disappeared from my view. But then I saw Anthony's body. It was moving. I put my hand on Nico's arm, but he held up his palm. That's when I saw what he was looking at. The big cat was tugging on Anthony's body, dragging it somewhere where it could have a feast.

I leaned over and threw up, silently and quickly.

"I think we are safe to turn and run now," Nico said.

I didn't wait for him to say it twice.

I ran as fast as I could until I emerged out onto the row of houses and then down to the beach and onto the dock, my feet pounding loudly.

Nico had stopped back by the houses. I turned and saw he was talking to a few people. They were nodding and then shaking their heads. Nico handed them something. It looked like business cards. And then he turned toward me. We sat on the dock, swinging our legs until the boat came back.

I didn't speak. Neither did he.

Finally, when I was safely in the boat, I said. "What were you talking to those people about?"

"I told them the cat had eaten my friend, and they should probably put up an electric fence or something to keep them safe in case the cat developed a taste for human flesh."

"Is that true? Will he want to eat people now?"

"I have no clue," Nico said.

"Did you really say all that to them?"

He shot me a look. "Yeah. What did you think I was saying to them?"

"I don't know." And I was telling the truth.

"You ready to go home now?"

I closed my eyes and nodded.

Belize was an amazingly beautiful country. And someday I'd love to actually explore it. But, right then, all I wanted to do was go home. I wanted to be in my loft with Rosalie and Django tucked safely in my big comfy bed, and I wanted to sleep. For a very long time. Ten years at the minimum.

46

My flight back to America wasn't until the next day so we stayed one more night at Nico's. I slept soundly and woke to quiet. After I showered, I dressed in a coral sundress, and I headed downstairs barefoot from my bedroom in Nico's estate. Today, I was going home.

The coral dress felt odd but strangely good. I'd packed colorful items as part of my disguise. However, since Nico knew who I was from the start, I hadn't needed to keep up the ruse. But something about being in Mexico with its saturated colors everywhere, made me want to shed my all-black clothing.

As I stopped in the stone courtyard, I noticed it was unusually quiet. At first, a trickle of fear zinged through me. Where were the armed guards? Had something happened? Then I spotted one of the sentries sitting quietly at a corner of the dining room table with a cup of coffee before him. He was watching me. Unobtrusively. I smiled and he gave a curt nod and then looked down at the newspaper spread out before him. I suppose now that I was no longer a threat, they could go back to the silent-but-deadly role they normally held.

This was reassuring. The thought of a big scary armed man

following Rosalie everywhere she went in this house was awful. But now I was seeing how they normally acted. There, but not there.

I headed into the kitchen and started digging around. I wondered if Nico had house staff or just big men with guns. Either way, I could fend for myself as I always did. There was a moka pot on the stove, so I emptied the grounds and dug in the cupboard until I found coffee beans. The first cupboard I opened had about ten different bags to choose from. Of course Nico had coffee beans. We were in Mexico! Hello!

As my moka pot gurgled on the stove, I opened a small refrigerator. It was nearly empty. But I found a bowl of fresh fruit on the counter and grabbed both a banana and a mango to munch. I was washing the mango off at the kitchen sink when I saw something out the window above the sink.

The window overlooked the back yard with the pool.

Nico was crouched down near the pool, facing the jungle area by the guest cottage. The black panther stepped out of the bushes. I held my breath, watching as it bounded toward Nico.

I thought they'd said the big cat had been shot dead in the attack. Once it was close enough, Nico buried his face in the panther's fur. Then he drew back, and the panther began to lick his face repeatedly.

It was one of the most remarkable things I'd ever seen. They raced around the yard together playfully. The panther was smaller than I'd thought. About half the size of Nico. They rolled on the grass together. Then, the cat walked over to a large bowl and began to drink.

Nico stripped. He tugged off his shirt, kicked off his shoes, and dropped his pants. He stepped out of them and then dove into the pool. I watched, transfixed, taking bites out of the banana.

After several laps, he pulled himself out of the pool. The

panther had already disappeared back into the wooded area. That's when Nico's gaze wandered. And then landed on me. I waved like an idiot. A huge grin spread across his face.

He met me in the courtyard. I handed him a cup of coffee.

"What were you really saying to those people in Belize?"

He sighed. "I told them that I was sending men to install an electric fence separating their land from the jungle because a beautiful panther lived there, and I didn't want any of them to accidentally stumble upon the animal and get harmed."

I frowned. It made sense. But why would they agree?

"Did you tell them about Anthony?"

"No. I told them that he had been watching my house for me and that I would be back soon to visit and hold a giant party to meet everyone."

"Hmmm." I said. It all sounded odd to me. "Why would you do that?"

"I'm the owner of the compound."

"You are?"

"Apparently. Anthony bought it in my name. He was attempting to transfer it to his own name, but it was still mine when he...died."

"Are you really going to go back?"

"Of course. I said I would. I am a man of my word."

I nodded.

"Did that make you afraid of your own cat? Seeing what the leopard did to Anthony?"

"Not at all," he said and scoffed. "I raised Tabitha since she was a baby. She is a wild animal, though, and I respect that. That's why I'm going to turn her over to the zoo now. There are two other panthers there, and the space has been renovated and expanded. I believe she will be much happier there in the company of other cats. Did you see how lonely she is? She was so excited to see me. It breaks my heart."

"And it will be safer for Rosalie to visit here, right?"

He winked. "And that is the main reason. Yes."

He took a big gulp of his coffee.

"Oh, this tastes wonderful," he said.

"Always tastes better when someone else makes it," I said.

He shrugged. "I wouldn't usually know."

His voice was low and matter-of-fact. I didn't think he was trying to garner sympathy.

But it made me realize he was probably a pretty lonely person.

"I've done a lot of thinking, and I have an idea I want to run by you about how we might proceed from here," I said.

We spent the next hour discussing the possibilities of my plan. He'd said a car was on its way to take me to the airport. Our visit would soon be over.

"I have to pack," I said, standing.

He gave me a look. I knew it might be the last time we ever had sex, since the next time I saw him Rosalie would be there.

"I might need some help."

On the way up to the room, he texted the car service and told them to come an hour later than planned.

Later, I packed while he still was in bed. When I was done, I looked over at him. He was staring straight up at the ceiling. His brow was furrowed.

"You aren't happy with our plan?" I needed to know right then, before I let him into Rosalie's life.

He turned toward me. "No, I am happy with it. It is for the best."

"Yes, it is."

Then he stared at me so intensely, I squirmed.

"I need to tell you something."

My heart raced.

"Anthony said that Rosalie wasn't mine. That she was not my child. That is how he lured me to Mexico City that day."

I stared back. He was leaving it up to me. He was giving me an out.

"What do you think?" I asked.

"I am afraid."

I could tell it had cost him a lot of effort to say those words.

"Well," I said, exhaling loudly. "She looks just like you."

He blinked and then blinked again.

"Really," I said. "If you need more proof, I guess we can arrange it. But only if she agrees."

"No, no, I don't need proof."

"Okay then," I said.

His phone dinged. He grabbed it off the nightstand.

"The car is here to take you to the airport."

I quickly grabbed my bag and turned toward the door.

Before I could reach it, he'd slipped out of bed and was right in front of me, blocking my way. Then his good arm wrapped around my head and gently brought my face forward until his lips met mine. I was relieved to be leaving. I didn't like it when my body wanted something so badly that it messed with my head. I needed to be in control. Especially when it came to making decisions about Rosalie.

I drew back and ducked around him without speaking. I was too afraid of what he might hear in my voice.

"I will see you next week," he said.

In the car to the airport, I realized I was excited to get home.

I only hoped that by putting some serious miles between me and Nico, he would lose his power over me.

47

AFTER I BOARDED MY FLIGHT TO SAN FRANCISCO, I CLOSED MY eyes to avoid having a conversation with the chatty Midwesterner beside me. She had a layover in my city and then a flight back to Minneapolis.

I needed some time to try to process everything that had happened over the past week.

Although I had killed before, it hadn't seemed as senseless and violent as the deaths of the three people at Dante's house. I had thought they were there to kill me and take Rosalie, but now I realized that Nico had ordered them to take me alive. And that was probably the only reason I *was* still alive. But they were dead.

It was something that was hard to swallow. It was something that I would have to live with forever. And it also made me wary to judge Nico. Who was I to judge his actions when I was a stone-cold killer, the same as he was?

We sat on that beach and tried to kill those two men. Sure, they were trying to kill us, but did we hesitate for one second? No. I had become something so foreign, so strange to myself, that I felt disoriented.

What had become of the girl who moved to San Francisco to embark on a life of debauchery? The worst I'd done was drink too much, sleep around too much, and smoke a little weed.

Now I'd become something else entirely.

I could say it wasn't my fault. I could say that I'd been forced to become a killer when someone had killed my family and tried to kill me. But in the end, it still boiled down to choices I'd made.

In a way, my strange relationship with Nico was comforting and natural in a way that I'd never experienced before. I didn't have to hide any part of me. With Bobby, the most pure-hearted man I'd ever loved and the man I would've stayed with until I was gray and old, I could never let him see the side of me that was a killer. It was a part of me I kept closed off, shut tight away from him. With the other man in my life—my other great love, James—it had been what had destroyed us. He was a police officer. I was essentially a criminal. Even though we'd come together in a beautiful way for such a wonderful time in my life, our destiny was to remain forever at odds. I'd only just recently started to feel like maybe we could be friends again.

But with *El Jefe Grande*—Nico Ortiz Morales—it was different. We were kindred spirits. Killers, yes. But only because of the circumstances life had thrown at us.

Soon, I would be in San Francisco. I was planning on meeting Dante and Rosalie there. Our flights were getting in at similar times. I could not wait to hug them both. And a small part of me was excited for them to meet Nico, which surprised me.

Maybe, just maybe, it would work. Rosalie had a right to know her father. If it went badly, then all bets were off. I didn't care how comfortable I felt around Nico. If Rosalie wasn't comfortable and didn't want him in her life, I would fight to ensure she didn't have to.

But when I'd seen him with the panther, I'd seen a playful side of him that was just what a father should be. It was reassuring.

With this thought, I let myself fully relax, pressing my head against the wall of the airplane and drifted off into a deep, calming sleep.

48

Since our return from Mexico, we'd settled back into our normal routine.

I walked Rosalie to school every day with Django and then went to work out at the dojo. As much as I wanted to tell Kato what was going on and why I'd fled to Mexico, I wasn't quite ready for it yet.

He was never one to pry, but I could tell he was curious by the way he looked at me during our training sessions.

I spent my days with Dante, who was staying with us while his house was being repaired. Plus, I wanted him there to meet Nico and weigh in.

Today was the day he was expected to arrive. I'd received a text and knew that I should expect him. It'd said, "Mexican avocados make the best guacamole."

Dante was busy in the kitchen preparing a feast—one of his most popular dishes from his restaurant. I could tell he missed his restaurant. I was proud that he'd been able to delegate the running of it for so long. It'd been the longest he'd been away from it.

Cooking in the kitchen was the happiest I'd seen him in a

long time. Except for the time he spent with Rosalie. He was always down on the floor with her, building Lego cities, or on the couch side-by-side playing with their iPads, building Minecraft villages. He really loved spending time with her, and it filled my heart with joy.

I glanced at my watch for the millionth time that afternoon.

It was time. He should be arriving any second.

Telling Rosalie and Dante I'd be right back, I went up to the roof. By leaning over the small, chest-high wall that surrounded my rooftop haven, I could see the street below.

He was late. Five minutes late.

Instead of being happy he might not show, I was disappointed. That emotion surprised me. It was a combination of wanting to see him again and finally coming to terms with the idea that maybe he was right—maybe Rosalie deserved a chance to get to know her father.

But as I stared down at the dark street, I began to notice small movements. There were people in the shadows below. A slight shimmer of light from a darkened doorway across the street. A silhouette by a building on the corner. Another two figures sitting in a car parked below.

For a second my blood ran cold. They were either Nico's advance security crew or they were his enemies coming to take him out in front of my home.

Then, to my surprise, instead of a black livery car or even a limousine or armored vehicle, a beat-up San Francisco cab pulled in front of my building. I held my breath as the door swung open and Nico climbed out. Part of me was waiting for gunfire to echo through the silent night. When it didn't, I relaxed. The men below were part of his security crew.

If I hadn't spent the previous week memorizing his body, I probably wouldn't have known it was him getting out of the cab. To anyone else, he looked like an older man wearing a stocking cap and heavy work boots. I pressed a button on my phone and spoke through the intercom when I saw him reach the front steps. "The door will open. Take the stairs to the top floor. I will meet you there."

I clicked open my front door with another button. I waited until the cab pulled away, and then I headed downstairs to greet Nico.

Inside my loft, the door to Rosalie's bedroom was open. She was dressed in a pink nightgown and her long dark hair was still slightly damp from her earlier bath. She was sitting crossed leg on the floor playing with her Barbie house, talking to herself as she made the dolls interact. Django lay lazily by her side with his eyes closed, his nose pressed up against one of her legs.

I poked my head in. "We're going to have a visitor tonight, remember?"

"Yes," she said without turning toward me. She was very busy playing. An adult visitor was boring, apparently. She kept her cheery chatter going, but Django raised his ears and turned to look at me. I swear sometimes I thought that damn dog understood everything I said.

I opened the front door and waited. I heard footsteps growing closer. Then I saw a stocking capped head followed by his face. His dark eyes flashed with what looked like genuine happiness to see me.

"Gia," he said. He leaned in to kiss my mouth, and I quickly turned my head so his lips landed on my cheek. I didn't know if Rosalie was watching. The sudden rumble of Django's growl behind me made Nico draw back suddenly. The dog was standing in Rosalie's doorway with every hair on his body bristling and his teeth bared.

"*Non fa niente*," I said. *That's all right.* He instantly relaxed.

"Come in," I said to Nico. Once the door was closed and

secured behind him, he crouched to his knees and then looked up at me.

"May I?"

"Django, he's a friend." My dog wagged his tail at the words.

"Come here, boy," Nico said.

Django ran over and smelled him and then wriggled his entire body in delight as Nico pet him roughly and praised him. "You are such a big bad ferocious beast!"

I laughed.

Then I noticed Nico had stood and was looking over my shoulder with his mouth wide open. I turned.

Rosalie stood in the doorway of her bedroom, holding one of her dolls, staring at Nico.

My mouth was suddenly dry.

"Rosalie, this is Nico Ortiz Morales."

She stared at him, biting her lip.

He crouched down again and spoke to her in Spanish.

Her brow furrowed. He kept talking. It was something about how he'd been friends with her mother. Her eyes grew wide.

"Would you like me to tell you more about her?"

"Yes, please," she said and walked over. He pointed at my couch.

"Shall we sit and talk?"

She nodded and pulled herself up on the couch. He sat down and Django jumped up on the couch between them. He spoke absentmindedly, petting Django as he did. He was still speaking Spanish. Rosalie's attention was rapt. I headed into the kitchen area and poured a shot of bourbon. I swallowed it and then poured another.

Dante was beside me, pouring his own drink, a small glass of Frangelico.

He downed it before speaking.

We couldn't make out what Nico was saying, but Rosalie was smiling.

"This is surreal," I said.

"I'll say."

After a few minutes, my door buzzed.

Dante looked up in surprise.

"It's James."

Dante's eyebrows practically disappeared into his hairline. "And I thought it couldn't get any weirder around here."

"You ain't seen nothing yet," I said.

The elevator doors slid open, revealing James in his wheelchair. Rosalie and Nico stood.

Rosalie ran and jumped into James's lap, wrapping her arms around him and kissing his face.

He loved her. She loved him. It was simple and pure.

It still broke my heart to see him having to use the wheelchair. His legs were still too weak for him to walk. He was in full-time physical therapy, getting disability from the police department, which had hired him back and told him he could start work whenever he was ready. He worked there part-time and did PT another several hours each day. He was a busy guy, but he always made time for Rosalie.

I introduced James to Nico.

"This is James. He's been a big part of Rosalie's life from the first day she came here."

"Thank you," he said, thrusting his hand out to James, who shook it heartily but kept his eyes trained on Nico's face.

"Rosalie," Nico said turning toward her. "It must be nice to have a police officer for such a good friend."

"Yes," she said and seemed uncertain.

I was not surprised that he knew who—and what —James was.

"That's why you always have to listen to what he says, right?"

"I do," Rosalie said grinning at James.

"Except when I tell you to let me win at chess," James said. "You are not a very good listener then. Not at all."

"Rosalie, why don't you, me, and Dante take Django up on the roof for a little bit," I said.

"But I want to see James," she said frowning.

"He's staying for dinner. We ordered take out from Katrina's."

"I want to stay down here," she said.

I wanted Nico and James to talk alone. "But Django really wants to play ball, don't you buddy?"

He whined with excitement. It was dirty pool invoking the "B" word. He wouldn't accept anything less now.

"Okay. Fine," Rosalie said, but she cast a longing glance back at James as we headed toward the stairwell.

On the roof, Rosalie threw a tennis ball as Django raced to get it and bring it back to her. The rooftop was lit with sparkling lights strung along the pergola and another string of lights along the chest-high wall of the roof. Dante and I watched them for a minute and then turned to face the dark.

Dante and I faced the Golden Gate Bridge to the north.

"What do you think?" I said.

"He clearly cares about Rosalie and seems to be good with her."

"Yes..." I trailed off.

"What is your main objection to him being in her life? Is it because you are worried she will be in danger? Because I don't think she's in any more danger with him than with you."

"Thanks."

"No, really. His security is pretty fucking tight," he said. "Look."

Down below, there were two armed men in front of my building. At least two cars on my street had shadowy figures inside—also his men.

"He needs that because more people want him dead than want me dead."

"Well, that's a switch," Dante said and, with a wink, nudged me.

"I'll see what James says."

"If he gives his blessing, is it a done deal?"

"I don't know. What do you think?"

Dante turned and watched Rosalie with Django.

"I think it needs to be up to her."

"She's too young to make that decision," I said, but wasn't convinced of my own words.

"What else?"

"He's killed dozens of people. Maybe indirectly, but still," I said.

"How many people have you killed, Gia?"

I didn't answer.

Stalemate.

49

Rosalie was leaving to go see her father. Alone for the first time.

It was the third visit for her. The first two I'd gone with her.

During the last one, we'd told her the truth. That he was her father.

At first, she hadn't said a word, and he'd looked over at me in anguish.

But then she nodded and said, "Okay."

And that was the last she'd spoken about it.

"Rosalie?" I said now. "What do you think about Nico being your dad?" I winced internally as I asked, but it needed to be said. I'd put off asking for far too long.

"It's okay," she said. "He's nice."

Well, it wasn't a fucking ringing endorsement, that's for sure.

He'd made me promise to double check with her that she was okay with visiting him alone and was okay with him being her father. That he needed to know this before we left made me like him more.

Over the past few months, with our two separate visits, I'd grown more comfortable with the idea of Rosalie spending time with him. If this two-week visit went well, the next one would be longer. Maybe by next summer, I'd consider letting her go for the entire month he'd hoped for. But I realized he was just as hesitant to rush things as I was.

"I promise you," he'd said on the phone the night before. "If she wants, I will get on a plane with her immediately to bring her home to you. She only needs to say the word."

"I believe you," I said.

"Good," he said. He cleared his throat. "I should go. I have an appointment."

I was surprised that his words made me jealous. Was it with a woman?

"It's eight at night," I said lightly.

"Yes, it is."

I swallowed. Well, fuck him.

"Gia?" he said.

"What?" I sighed.

"I miss you."

I closed my eyes. *Me too.*

But I refused to say the words out loud.

"Have a good night," I said and hung up.

Now, in Rosalie's bedroom, packing her small suitcase and backpack, my stomach was doing flip flops. So far both of our trips had been a blast.

The first time we'd gone to the beach house.

Every day, Nico's men would clear the beach, and we would spend the day there under big umbrellas on lounge chairs while Rosalie played in the waves.

You'd think she'd get sick of the water. Nope. Girl was a fish. Or a mermaid, if you asked her.

Half the time, Nico was in the waves with her, teaching her to body surf, or playing catch with her and Django. The damn dog loved the water as much as Rosalie. It was surprising.

He would bark at the waves coming in and then run over and try to bite them.

Then he would rush into the water and paddle with his tail sticking straight up and wagging furiously.

It was comical.

I was happy Django was there. He was an added layer of protection. That dog would kill anyone who tried to get at Rosalie.

The second time, we'd also brought Django and stayed in Nico's house in San Miguel de Allende. There, we visited museums and the opera and funky art galleries and pottery studios.

Rosalie spoke Spanish with everyone, and it was heart-warming to see how fascinated she was with the museum exhibit about the indigenous people of Central America.

She didn't seem to mind traveling everywhere with a pack of armed guards. She'd turned them to mush under her smile. It was the first time I saw any sign of humanity from them. I was glad. They'd have more than just a business interest in keeping her safe. She brought a level of life and joy to that house that I hadn't thought possible.

But now she was going on her own. I would accompany her on a private plane to Mexico City where Nico would meet us, and I'd turn her over to him and then fly back.

————

IN MEXICO CITY, our private jet was met by a rolling staircase.

I held Rosalie's hand as we went down the stairs.

Nico was waiting in a big black car. As soon as we were halfway down the stairs, he got out and stood there grinning. He was a damn good looking man.

Rosalie ran to him and hugged him and then drew back with an embarrassed look on her face.

I walked up and he kissed me on both cheeks and then on the mouth, quickly. I laughed in surprise.

"Sorry, couldn't resist," he said.

I was about to say "tease," but looked down at Rosalie who was watching us.

"Gia, why can't you stay, too?" she said. I was suddenly worried. Didn't she want to be here?

I crouched down before I spoke, but Nico beat me to it.

"Are you sure you're okay staying by yourself? You can go back home with Gia. I don't mind." He had a smile in his voice, trying to reassure her.

"No, I want to stay. I want Gia to stay, too."

"Gia?" Nico said. "You are more than welcome to stay."

I was confused. The whole point was getting Rosalie ready to stay with him for part of the year, wasn't it? Alone.

"Honey, let's try you staying by yourself this time," I said.

"Okay."

"You sure?"

She nodded. "I will miss you."

"I'll miss you, too." I buried my face in her hair and hugged her tightly.

"Maybe next time I'll come to San Francisco again and you can show me around?" he said.

"Maybe," I said. I crouched down and gave Rosalie a hug.

"You call me anytime," I said. "Have fun, Sweetie."

"Okay," she said.

I turned before she could see my face.

Damn, this was harder than I thought it would be.

On the plane, I watched as the black car drove away and fought my instincts to race out of the plane and chase after it.

She was not mine. I was only there to guide her and help her grow into an adult. She did not belong to me. No more than she belonged to Nico.

But we would do everything in our power to keep her safe and help raise her into an adult who was powerful and happy and confident and content.

Even though we lived in separate worlds and had separate lives, Nico and I had an unbreakable bond: a beautiful, spirited child we both loved deeply.

That was a bond we'd always share.

I fell asleep on the plane comforted by this thought.

———

THE LOFT WAS quiet and lonely without Rosalie. Django had stayed home this time, and I was glad, but he paced and whined, poking his head in her room frequently to look for her.

"She'll be back," I'd say trying to reassure him.

Poor baby didn't understand.

Dante called to make sure I was okay.

"I can come down," he said. "Just say the word."

"Maybe this weekend. I'm going to dinner with James tomorrow."

"Oh yeah."

"At his house," I said. As I said the words, I realized I was nervous.

"Wow."

"Right?"

"To meet the wife?"

"And baby."

"When you get home, call me immediately. I don't care how late it is," he said.

I laughed. "It's not that big of a deal." James and I had established a tentative friendship since Nico's visit.

"The hell it's not."

"Stop," I said. "You're freaking me out."

The next day, I'd gone through about a dozen outfits before settling on my trusty faded black jeans, a white T-shirt, a black blazer, and black combat boots. I'd tried on and discarded my worn-in leather pants and a series of black dresses before just putting on basically what I wore every day. The blazer was sort of fancy, wasn't it? I just hoped that his wife didn't answer the door in a dress and pearls.

Then again, if she did, we didn't have a chance in hell of finding common ground anyway, right?

I was terrified to meet the woman who had snagged James.

Even though the timeline didn't support the theory 100 percent, the reality was that he'd ditched me and had fallen in love with her. Enough to marry her and have a baby right away.

It stung, but I no longer was in love with James.

For some reason having the affair with Nico had made me realize I could have red-hot sex like that with someone else. And that there were other men out there for me to be obsessed with.

I didn't want to admit it, but I spent a crazy amount of time thinking about Nico. Daydreaming about what our lives might be like together. Me at his side. It was absurd. And, frankly, embarrassing. And, honestly, impossible.

I had my life in San Francisco. He had his in Mexico. Period. End of story.

I had two shots of tequila in the backseat of the car I'd hired before I got out in front of James's house in South San Francisco.

His wife greeted me at the door with a hug.

"I'm so happy to finally meet you," she said. Her smile was genuine. She wore black leggings and a hoodie. Her hair was pulled back in a messy ponytail, but she had pink lipstick on. She was pretty and down to earth. Unpretentious. Genuine.

I wanted to be bitchy, but I couldn't help but smile back.

In the living room, James was sitting on the floor with the baby. I watched as he hoisted himself up to a chair. His wife, Genevieve, leaned down and scooped up the baby, handing her to me. She was a nurse. James had met her in Germany. And wanted her instead of me. Despite this, I couldn't help but like her.

I held on to the squirming bundle in my arms for dear life, shooting an alarmed glance at James. He burst into laughter.

"Sit down," he said, gesturing to the chair beside his.

I did. Once I was seated, I felt more at ease, so I shifted the baby so she was sitting in my lap. She cooed and drooled, and I jiggled my leg, hoping I was doing everything right.

So far, she wasn't crying so I considered that a good sign.

"I'm glad to see you found someone," he said after Genevieve left the room.

"What are you talking about?" I scowled.

"Gia, you clearly have a thing with him," he'd laughed. "It's so obvious."

"We *had* a thing. It's over."

"I doubt that," he'd said.

"Well, it's over now. It's not like we're ever going to do anything ever again. Not with Rosalie in the picture. Plus, he's like my grandpa's age. If I had a grandpa."

"He's not that much older," James had said. "Whatever. You're just looking for an excuse to not be happy because you don't think you deserve it. I know this song and dance, Gia."

I glared at him.

Just then, his perfect wife walked in and dried her hands on her pants before taking the baby from me with a smile.

"You guys hungry?"

50

It had been a long-ass week since Rosalie had left.

After having dinner with James, I'd spent the next three days alone.

On the fourth day, I dragged myself up and out of the house to the dojo.

Kato was on vacation to Canada with his family, so I worked out with his replacement. It was not satisfying. But I realized it was because I'd been looking for friendship, not a workout. I was lonely.

Darling was watching her grandbaby in the East Bay. When I tried to talk to her, we'd been interrupted by the baby howling. "Gotta go, Gia."

Dante was busy with a special event at his restaurant.

I'd considered going up there but decided against it. He'd be too busy to socialize.

For a crazy second, I'd even considered calling Eva but for some reason felt embarrassed. What was I going to say to her: "Hi?"

Finally, I dialed Nico. It was eleven at night.

"Gia? Is everything okay?"

"Yes. Sorry. I just wanted to talk," I said.

He was quiet for a few seconds. Then he cleared his throat.

"I'm too old for you."

"*What*?" I was taken aback.

"You need someone who is young and whom you can have your own children with one day."

"I don't know what you're talking about."

"Gia," he said, and his voice was so soft I cringed.

"We will always be a part of each other's lives now. That is enough."

"I don't think it is," I said. The words tumbled out before I realized it.

"It must be."

I felt a lump in my throat. He was right. Our lives would never intertwine except for the brief periods each year when we got together for Rosalie's sake.

"I wish it could be different," I said, closing my eyes as I spoke. I was astonished that I could make myself this vulnerable in front of a man.

"Me, too," he said. "We have…something special. It's a chemistry, yes, but it's deeper than that."

"Yes," I said. An inexplicable joy filled me, knowing he felt the same way I did. He knew it, too.

"In another life. In another time."

I was openly crying now. It was the story of my life.

If only. In another life. In another time.

"Why don't you come down here," he said. "For a visit. I never got to show you all the wonders of my country.

I didn't know what to say.

"Gia? Will you come? For a long weekend?"

"Yes. Yes, I'll come."

"I'll send a car for you first thing in the morning."

I smiled and hung up.

. . .

The story continues in *Cold As Death*, the next Gia Santella Thriller. Head to the next page for a sneak peek or order today by clicking the link or scanning the QR code below!
www.amazon.com/B07Y8RSG5G

Stay up to date with Kristi Belcamino's new releases by clicking the link or scanning the QR code below!
(You'll receive a **free** copy of *First Vengeance: A Gia Santella Prequel!*)
https://liquidmind.media/kristi-belcamino-newsletter-signup-1-first-vengeance/

Did you enjoy *Stone Cold?* Click the link or scan the QR code below to let us know your thoughts!
www.amazon.com//B07Y9VKN2P

COLD AS DEATH CHAPTER ONE

Nico Morales stood in front of the vanity mirror and adjusted the cuffs of his white shirt. He wore the ruby cufflinks that Gia had given him for his birthday the month before. Their blood red color was a sharp contrast to the shirt and black tuxedo.

Gia sat before him on a pink velvet tufted chair pulled up to the vanity, applying red lipstick. It was the only thing she wore.

After she pressed her lips together to set the lipstick, Gia leaned forward and swiped a black pencil along her upper lash line.

Morales groaned.

"Stop it," he growled. "You're going to make us late."

"Me?" she said with feigned innocence.

"If you don't get dressed now, I'm going to pick you up and take you to bed and then you won't have time to get ready and will have to go naked."

"Perfect," she said, holding his gaze in the mirror and stretching like a cat.

"Damn you."

She looked away, but he caught her smile.

He leaned down and scooped her up into his arms. She

giggled and pretended to fight him off as he carried her to the bed.

Later, after he was dressed again, she sat back down at the vanity. This time she'd managed to put on red silk panties and a bra.

"We're going to be late," he said.

"What else is new," she said, brushing her silky dark hair. "Hand me a dress."

He paused in the large walk in closet and winced at the number of choices.

"Just grab the closest one," she hollered from the bedroom.

He tugged one of the dresses off a hanger and stepped out of the closet holding a slippery flip of fabric.

"Toss it here," Gia said.

She stood and caught it and tugged the silver fabric over her head.

She slid her feet into some sandals, grabbed a small bag and headed for the door.

"Let's go," she said.

"That's it?" he asked. "You're ready?"

Instead of answering, she left the bedroom and pressed the button for the elevator.

He shook his head. That woman always kept him guessing. Just when he thought she might be predictable, she'd shatter all his preconceived notions.

Sylvia, his dead wife, used to take at least four hours to prepare for a night at the opera. But Gia Santella would take ten minutes to apply makeup, five minutes to get dressed, and was out the door. He smiled. And she would still look better than everyone else in the entire place.

Downstairs, Nico's daughter, Rosalie, sat at the bar in the kitchen, head bent over a stack of math problems, her brow furrowed in concentration. Rosalie's dog, Django, lay at her feet, his head resting on his paws. His black eyes darted up at Nico, but the rest of his body stayed still. Django had been Gia's dog. She'd rescued him from a drug dealer who was beating him. Gia had kicked the shit out of the man and taken the dog home.

Django was a Pitbull mix and docile as a sloth. Until you tried to mess with his family.

When Gia had taken Rosalie in, the dog made it his priority to watch out for the girl. It was as if he sensed that she had been dealt a rough hand in life—seeing her mother and almost all of the rest of her family murdered in front of her and then witnessing numerous other people being slaughtered as she made her way to America.

Rosalie was a surprisingly optimistic and happy child despite all of it. When she saw Nico walk in with Gia, Rosalie jumped off the barstool and ran to him. He scooped her up in his arms.

Rosalie's tutor and nanny, Camila, looked up at the couple. "Have a wonderful time," she said. "Django and I have it all under control here."

Once Rosalie disengaged from her father, Gia leaned down to kiss the top of the girl's silky black head. "Don't forget to take a bath tonight and only three chapters of your book before lights out, okay? We have swim lessons early tomorrow morning."

Rosalie pursed her tiny pink lips together in an expression of disappointment but nodded grudgingly. Then she turned to Nico.

"Daddy, when am I going to be old enough to go to the opera with you?"

Nico looked over her head at Gia with surprise.

"I didn't know you wanted to," he said, crouching down to Rosalie's level and looked into her long-lashed dark eyes, replicas of his.

"Yes, I very much do."

"Hmm," he said. "School nights are not the best, but I'm sure we can find one on the weekend or during break."

He hugged her and lifted her back up onto the barstool. "Be good for Camila while we're gone."

"I always am," she said tossing her hair. Her precociousness made him grin.

As they climbed into the back of the car, Nico thought that everything about his life made him smile. His daughter, the love of his life, had grown to love him after not knowing him for the first eight years of her life. Gia Santella, a beautiful woman whom he was crazy about, thought he wasn't half bad. He had more money than he could ever spend in ten lifetimes. And he was strong and fit. He had health, wealth, and love. He was one lucky man.

COLD AS DEATH CHAPTER TWO

Sitting in the dark snuggled in my white faux fur coat, I snaked my fingers along Nico's leg seductively, dragging them along his inner thigh toward his groin.

I kept my eyes wide and glued on the performance below. All innocence over here.

Nico plucked my hand off his leg, firmly placed it in my own lap, and patted it like I was a five-year-old.

I'd try a sneak attack instead. Something a little harder for him to resist. This time I didn't bother with the leg. I wriggled in my seat, subtly scrunching up the silky fabric of my dress until the thigh closest to him was completely bare. I snuck a glance at the elderly woman to my left, but she was concentrating on the stage below. It was quite dark in the upper portion of the theater where we were sitting, which was what I was counting on. I innocently reached for Nico's hand and he willingly took it. Before he could react, I maneuvered his hand up my bare thigh and under my dress, shoving it against my red silk panties. He groaned loudly and jerked his hand back.

I tried to stifle my laugh. The woman beside me glanced

over. It was too dark to see her expression, but I was fairly certain she was giving me a dirty look.

"Sorry," I whispered.

Then I leaned over and spoke in Nico's ear. "I can't help it. This scene always makes me horny."

He grabbed my hand, pulled me to standing, and led me toward the aisle. People shot us looks as we made our way for the exit. In the lobby, I turned to wrap my arms around Nico's neck. "Let's get out of here. There's a hotel across the street."

He smiled down at me. "Jesus, Gia, I can't take you anywhere."

"You can take me anywhere," I said. "As long as there is a bed."

"Like you need one?"

"You're right," I said, holding his hand as we headed for the door. "I stand corrected. As long as there is a smidgen of privacy."

"Just a smidgen?"

"Yeah. I mean I'm not shy, but *you* have a reputation to uphold."

As I spoke, the valet rushed over. "Mr. Morales—" he began.

Nico held up his palm. "Fernando, we aren't leaving quite yet."

"Yes, sir," the valet said and retreated back to his little stand.

Holding my hand, Nico looked both ways and when traffic parted, he led me across the street to a hotel with a red carpet and fancy awning. Inside, at the front desk, a young man frowned when he saw us.

"I'm sorry, we don't have any vacancies."

But then when we drew closer, his cheeks reddened.

"My apologies Mr. Morales. The penthouse suite is ready for you."

He slid a keycard over the desk without another word.

Nico picked up the card and left a thick wad of money in its place.

In the elevator, Nico kissed me hard, pressing me up against the mirrored wall. I reached over and hit the stop button. His eyes grew wide.

As I worked the belt loose on his pants, he exhaled in exaggeration and said, "Gia, I don't know if you are going to extend my life or make me die young."

I shrugged. "You only live once, sailor."

Are you loving *Cold As Death*? Scan the QR code below to order your copy today!

ALSO BY KRISTI BELCAMINO

Enjoying Kristi Belcamino? Scan the code below to see her Amazon Author page!

Gia Santella Crime Thriller Series

Vendetta

Vigilante

Vengeance

Black Widow

Day of the Dead

Border Line

Night Fall

Stone Cold

Cold as Death

Cold Blooded

Dark Shadows

Dark Vengeance

Dark Justice

Deadly Justice

Deadly Lies

Additional books in series:

Taste of Vengeance

Lone Raven

Vigilante Crime Series

Blood & Roses

Blood & Fire

Blood & Bone

Blood & Tears

Queen of Spades Thrillers

Queen of Spades

The One-Eyed Jack

The Suicide King

The Ace of Clubs

The Joker

The Wild Card

High Stakes

Poker Face

Standalone Novels

Coming For You

Sanctuary City

The Girl in the River

Buried Secrets

Dead Wrong (Young Adult Mystery)

Gabriella Giovanni Mystery Series

Blessed are the Dead

Blessed are the Meek

Blessed are Those Who Weep

Blessed are Those Who Mourn

Blessed are the Peacemakers

Blessed are the Merciful

Nonfiction

Letters from a Serial Killer

ALSO BY WITHOUT WARRANT

More Thriller Series from Without Warrant Authors

Dana Gray Mysteries by C.J. Cross

Girl Left Behind

Girl on the Hill

Girl in the Grave

The Kenzie Gilmore Series by Biba Pearce

Afterburn

Dead Heat

Heatwave

Burnout

Deep Heat

Fever Pitch

Storm Surge (Coming Soon)

Willow Grace FBI Thrillers by Anya Mora

Shadow of Grace

Condition of Grace (Coming Soon)

Gia Santella Crime Thriller Series
by Kristi Belcamino

Vendetta

Vigilante

Vengeance

Black Widow

Day of the Dead

Border Line

Night Fall

Stone Cold

Cold as Death

Cold Blooded

Dark Shadows

Dark Vengeance

Dark Justice

Deadly Justice

Deadly Lies

Vigilante Crime Series by Kristi Belcamino

Blood & Roses

Blood & Fire

Blood & Bone

Blood & Tears

Queen of Spades Thrillers by Kristi Belcamino

Queen of Spades

The One-Eyed Jack

The Suicide King

The Ace of Clubs

The Joker

The Wild Card

High Stakes

Poker Face

AUTHOR'S NOTE

When I was 16, I read Jackie Collins' book, *Lucky*, and it rocked my world. For the first time in my prolific reading life (yes, I was the kid holed up in my room reading as many books as I could as often as I could), I met a character who was not only Italian-American like me, but a strong, powerful, and successful badass woman who didn't take crap from anybody and loved to have sex!

Although I had dreamed of being a writer, it never seemed like a realistic dream and my attempts at writing seemed pitiful. So I studied journalism and became a reporter—it was a way to be a writer and have a steady paycheck.

It was only when I was in my forties that I got the guts to write a book. And it was a few years after that I was brave enough to write the character I really wanted to write—Gia Santella.

She's not Lucky Santangelo, of course. I mean, nobody could be as cool as Lucky is, but I like to think that maybe Gia and Lucky would have been friends.

Gia is my alter ego. The woman who does and says things I

never could or would, but whom I admire and would love to be friends with.

If you like her, I'm pretty sure we'd be the best of friends in real life!

x Kristi

ABOUT THE AUTHOR

Kristi Belcamino is a USA Today bestseller, an Agatha, Anthony, Barry & Macavity finalist, and an Italian Mama who bakes a tasty biscotti.

Her books feature strong, kickass, independent women facing unspeakable evil in order to seek justice for those unable to do so themselves.

In her former life, as an award-winning crime reporter at newspapers in California, she flew over Big Sur in an FA-18 jet with the Blue Angels, raced a Dodge Viper at Laguna Seca, attended barbecues at the morgue, and conversed with serial killers.

During her decade covering crime, Belcamino wrote and reported about many high-profile cases including the Laci Peterson murder and Chandra Levy disappearance. She has appeared on *Inside Edition* and local television shows. She now writes fiction and works part-time as a reporter covering the police beat for the St. Paul *Pioneer Press*.

Her work has appeared in such prominent publications as *Salon*, the *Miami Herald*, *San Jose Mercury News,* and *Chicago Tribune*.

facebook.com/kristibelcaminowriter

instagram.com/kristibelcaminobooks

tiktok.com/@kristibelcaminobooks